RUFF VS. FLUFF

A QUEENIE AND ARTHUR NOVEL

SPENCER QUINN

SCHOLASTIC PRESS • NEW YORK

All rights reserved. Published by Scholastic Press, an imprint of Scholastic Inc., *Publishers since 1920*. SCHOLASTIC, SCHOLASTIC PRESS, and associated logos are trademarks and/or registered trademarks of Scholastic Inc.

The publisher does not have any control over and does not assume any responsibility for author or third-party websites or their content.

Library of Congress Cataloging-in-Publication Data available

ISBN 978-1-338-09139-7

10 9 8 7 6 5 4 3 2 1   19 20 21 22 23

Printed in the U.S.A.   23
First edition, April 2019

Book design by Maeve Norton

TO ALL THE EPHS OUT THERE,
ESPECIALLY FAMILY EPHS—DAD,
LILY, JAKE, AND MADDY—AND
THE CLASS OF '68

ONE

QUEENIE

I HAVE THE MOST BEAUTIFUL VOICE. I USE it to say just one thing: *Me-ow!* Have you ever heard anything so lovely? And it starts with *me*! How great is that? I love starting with me. In fact, I have no time for anything that doesn't start with me and keep on going with me right until it ends, with me. Me—or actually ME—is how I think of myself, but you can call me Queenie, like all the other humans. Call me Queenie—but don't expect me to come, or perform some stupid trick, or pay the slightest attention to you. You have my permission to look at me all you want. I don't blame you. I'm a thing of beauty.

This is probably a good moment to describe myself. Where to even start? With my tail? Kind of cool, starting at the end. And I'm cool, no doubt about that. Mom always says, "That Queenie is one cool cat." Not my mom, who I really don't remember, but the kids' mom, who has another name I can't be bothered to come up with at the moment, and anyway, she's just Mom around these parts.

These parts are what humans call snow country, although we didn't have any snow yet and it was getting close to Christmas. I knew it was close to Christmas because Elrod hauled a big tree into the Big Room and, after a lot of grunting and fumbling around plus muttered words that won't be repeated here, got it set up in front of the fireplace. I myself was watching this performance from one of my favorite spots, namely on the top shelf of the bookcase in the corner. Books can be quite comfortable. Were you aware of that already? What do humans actually know? I'm afraid the true answer might disappoint.

Elrod's the handyman. Why? Because he's a man with hands? I had no interest in exploring the question. Humans have their ways, usually noisy, and we in the cat world have ours, usually quiet. At the moment I was absolutely motionless and silent, yet still somehow the main character. Meanwhile Elrod was admiring the tree and rubbing his hands together, meaning job well done.

Mom came into the room, stopping short when she saw the tree.

"Elrod?"

He turned to her. Elrod—a very big guy with a thick beard and a ponytail, a look you see a lot up here in snow country—moves kind of slow. Mom—a small woman with short, no-nonsense hair and real sharp eyes—moves kind of fast.

"Ma'am?" he said.

Mom blinked. Because she'd asked Elrod not to call her *ma'am* from the very first day he came here, and that was . . . who knew when? And here, so much later, he was still doing it? "It makes me feel old, Elrod," she always said. Although she didn't say it now. Instead she said, "The tree."

"Ain't she a beauty? Sixteen feet, six inches—measured it myself."

"Yes, but—"

"Guess how?"

"How what?"

This, like a lot of human talk, was failing to hold my complete attention. I curled up next to a nice soft paperback.

"How I did the measure. With an app on my phone!" Elrod slapped his thigh. The sound—like a gunshot at close range—knocked me clear out of the nap I was just sliding into. I eyed the worn woolen cap on Elrod's head, the one with the Bruins logo, and had an idea. I'm partial to wool.

"No flies on you," Mom said, which maybe didn't need saying at this time of year, when there were no flies anywhere, but I gave her a pass. I like Mom. She and I both have a thing for sardines. "The problem is the distance between the tree and the fireplace."

"Gotcha!" said Elrod, and took out his phone. "You want me to measure it?"

Mom usually keeps her voice nice and even. You learn to look for other things, like the way her foot was starting to tap. "I'm just remembering last year, Elrod."

"Last year? You mean when the, um . . ."

"Exactly. When the tree burst into flames."

Then came the sound of a tinkling bell from the front desk. The tinkling bell could mean the arrival of guests, and guests were what we had to have more of, which Mom had been saying a lot lately. She hurried out of the room and Elrod got busy.

Maybe now is when to mention that we own the Blackberry Hill Inn—we being me, Mom, and the twins, Harmony and Bro, and me, in case I missed getting me at the top of this list. Elrod's the handyman and Bertha's the cook, but she's just here in the mornings because breakfast is the only meal we serve. At one time there was also Dad, but then came a divorce for reasons I may have slept through, and now he was gone.

Mom came into the room, accompanied by a man trailing a suitcase on rollers.

"Elrod, this is Mr. LeMaire. He's from Montreal, Canada."

"Nice to meet you," Elrod said.

"Uh-huh," said Mr. LeMaire, a tall man, as tall as Elrod, but much thinner. In fact, kind of skinny, with a face that started narrow and got more so, the nose beak-like. Mom led him across the Big Room and up the broad stairs toward the guest rooms. They all have names, our guest rooms, possibly different kinds of berries or flowers, I forget which. It might even be . . . birds.

Birds. Why did I have to think of birds? Because of Mr. LeMaire's nose? That was probably it. I licked my paws for a while, trying to drive the thought of birds from my mind. Birds were the reason I didn't go outside much anymore. Where's the justice in that? When I catch a mouse behind the fridge, for example, all I hear is "Good job, Queenie! Way to go!" But when I catch a bird—much harder than catching a mouse, by the way, and lots more fun, especially if you nab them at the moment of takeoff!—why, then it's all about "Bad Queenie!" and "How could you do such a thing?" Sometimes I just don't get the credit I deserve. I licked my paws some more, even gnawed a bit, trying to gnaw birds right out of my mind. I ended up thinking about birds, birds, birds. What were those red ones? Cardinals? Couldn't be easier to spot, so what do they expect? Once, I was out in the yard, the backyard that slopes all the way past the woodpile and the apple orchard down to Blackberry Creek, only I was much closer to the house, actually hanging out near the bird feeder, when—

I heard a squeak coming from the front hall, the squeak of a rubber boot heel on the hardwood floor. I'm an expert at hearing squeaks you probably miss, and not only that but I can identify certain specific squeaks, the higher and squeakier the better. This particular squeak came from the heel of a green boot with red laces that belonged to Harmony. Have I mentioned her yet? She and Bro are the twins. They're my favorite humans in the world. I like them almost as much as I like me. Well, let's not get crazy. Bro's name actually may not be Bro, but that's what Harmony calls him and it caught on. I tried to remember the name he had before Bro and gave up, instead uncurling myself and enjoying a nice lazy stretch. What a lovely sight that must have been, but there was no one around to see it. Not even Elrod, now on his knees and peering under the lowest branches of the tree.

The next moment, Harmony came into the room, carrying a load of firewood and, yes, wearing her Christmas boots, the green ones with the red laces. You may think that being right all the time would get boring, but take it from me: It doesn't.

"Hey, Elrod," she said. "What a nice tree!"

Elrod, now lying facedown and way under the tree, just the lower part of his legs showing, squirmed around and said something muffled that sounded like, "Sixteen feet, six inches, Harmony! And you'll never guess how I—"

That was when the tree started getting tippy. I was down on the floor myself, headed toward Harmony with the idea of rubbing myself against her leg for a bit, just reminding her of me, but I'm not the type to stick around when catastrophe is in the air. Before you knew it—almost before I knew it—I'd leaped up to the top of the piano, a fine spot although not as cozy as the bookcase. How pleasant to be so quick!

Meanwhile, Harmony—who's pretty quick herself, in human terms—had somehow put down her load of split logs and grabbed on to a big branch of the tree, getting it back to almost steady.

"Uh, thanks, Harmony," Elrod said, backing out from underneath, butt first. I actually had one paw raised, all set to slink my way down to Harmony and get on with the leg-rubbing ritual, when familiar crashing and banging started up from the direction of the front door. In walked Bro, also with an armful of wood, but although far from quiet in his movements, Bro wasn't the chief noisemaker. That would be the final member of our household, whom I suppose I'll have to mention.

There he was, real as real could be, and just so excited to be in the mix, careening around in his undignified way, carrying one measly split log, and a small one at that, wedged crookedly in that drooling mouth of his. He was real proud to be helping out. That weird stubby tail wagging at blur speed was the giveaway. Here's a tip—all you ever need to know about Arthur you can tell from what that tail is up to. Forget about subtlety when it comes to Arthur. That's true of all dogs, although many of them are much more presentable than Arthur. Maybe all of them. For example, what's the deal with that gnarly coat of his, kind of like the old tweed jacket Elrod wears when he has to dress up? And do his ears really need to be that floppy, practically dragging on the floor? Plus don't get me started on his nose, which takes up about half his—

"Arthur! No! Stop!"

That was Harmony. But too late. Anything the slightest bit unusual—like the sight of Elrod crawling out from under the tree—is enough to get Arthur going. It was all so, so predictable: Arthur's sudden change of direction, ripping tufts of wool off Mom's favorite rug with his clumsy claws; then his all-paws-off-the-ground-at-once sprint toward Elrod, the split log dangling out one side of his mouth; followed by a series of Arthur-type decisions, all customarily demented; and ending with the tree toppling down on Elrod, Harmony, Bro, and a pretty crystal flower vase, Mom's favorite. But not on Arthur, who stood just outside the circle of destruction, his tail still wagging, although slower now, as though beginning to have doubts. I made a mental note concerning those tufts of rug wool, now readily available, then closed my eyes and settled into that nap, which was what I should have done from the start.

TWO

ARTHUR

AFTER SOME SORT OF FUSS IN THE Big Room, the details blurring quickly and then vanishing from my mind forever, I found myself in the kitchen. The kitchen was my favorite room in our whole house, or inn, or whatever it was. I've never been clear on that, which doesn't worry me in the least! Why worry? Whoa! I stopped right there, just inside the kitchen, because I'd been hit—from out of nowhere!—with a strange and bothersome thought. Maybe a pretty good reason to worry would be that things might not work out the way you want. Whoa and double whoa, whatever that means. I had no idea, but it's something Harmony says.

Bertha, standing by the stove—she's the cook, in case you don't know that already—glanced over in my direction. Bertha's big and strong and tough and loud, even kind of scary, but it was important to get along with her. Why? For a moment, I couldn't remember. Then it hit me: Bertha's the cook! What could be more important than getting along with the cook? Bertha just happened to be frying up some sausages. Sausages! It was the smell of sausages that had brought me here in the first place, from wherever I'd just been, possibly the Big Room.

"Hey, you big dope," Bertha said. "Something on your mind?"

On my mind? No, nothing, not a thing. Well, except for sausages. I wanted one desperately! Or more than one! All of them! Please! Now! I rolled over and played dead, my only trick.

"What makes you think you deserve a sausage?"

I lay on my back, all paws in the air, thinking my hardest. Why did I deserve a sausage? Because I loved them! There—the answer to the easiest question I'd ever heard!

"Know how dumb you look with that enormous tongue hanging out of your mouth?"

Another question? Hadn't I just answered one? I gave this new one a pass, not about to make a habit of answering every random question that came down the pike.

"G'wan," Bertha said. "Git." She jabbed her big fork into a sausage, sizzling in the pan, and flicked it my way. I caught it in midair—I can catch like you wouldn't believe, especially sausages—and hightailed it on out of there, actually twisting around to see if my tail was in fact high. And it was! Straight up and down! Ooo-ee, baby! I gobbled up that sausage—perhaps a touch on the warm side, but no one ever says old Arthur is hard to please—and raced upstairs for no reason at all, except that I felt great.

Upstairs is where the guests stay, here at the Blackberry Hill Inn. Up the main stairs is what I mean. Up the back stairs is for us, the family: Mom, Harmony, Bro, and me. Have I left anyone out? Not that I can think of.

It was nice and quiet upstairs, maybe not a good thing. Nice and quiet meant not many guests, and not many guests meant money problems, and money problems made Mom anxious, and that was bad. I love Mom. When she's anxious she stops and takes a deep breath. She'd been doing that a lot lately. And also staring up at the sky and saying, "We need snow, Arthur. Think snow." And I had! I'd thought snow my very hardest, thinking snow, snow, snow! But not a single flake came down, the sky remaining clear and blue.

So there I was, feeling bad for Mom but great about everything else while I pitter-pattered down the hall past the guest rooms, no fresh human smell easing out from under any of the closed doors, meaning no guests. I did catch a fairly recent whiff of . . . how to put this? Another sort of member of the family I'd possibly left out when I was naming everybody? Maybe better that way. I forgot all about her—and her sharp claws! and her slinky ways! and her golden eyes, so mean and strange!—and headed down to the end of the hall. The last guest room door was not totally closed, and through the opening came the scent of a human male. Nothing unusual except that this particular human male smell was heavy on the earwax. Elrod's smell has only a hint of earwax, and Bro's none at all. Meaning this was worth a quick peek. I pushed the door open a little more and stuck my head inside.

The room at the end of the hall was one of the nicest we had, with a king-sized bed—which I've lain on once or twice when no one was around, but that's a secret—a balcony, and a view of Mount Misty. The man in the room—a stranger to me, a narrow-faced dude with a nose both big and thin at the same time, sort of like an ax blade, actually—sat at the desk. He seemed to be studying some sort of map. I knew maps. Lots of hikers and snowshoers turn up here—snow! snow! snow!—and they've always got their faces in maps. This one seemed different from the others I'd seen, all in pencil for one thing, plus the paper smelled kind of old, for another. Ax-Nose Man took out a red pen and made a small circle on the map before folding it up and putting it in his pocket. Then he went to the bed, where a suitcase lay open. He fished through some clothes inside and pulled out . . . What was this? A gun? Yes. Specifically a handgun, kind of old and beat-up-looking.

We get hunters here in the fall, but they carry rifles and shotguns. I've been out with the hunters once or twice, but it ends up being a little too exciting. But what I'm trying to get across is that we don't see much in the way of handguns. And wasn't hunting season over? I thought I'd heard something about that from Bertha, one of the best hunters in the state, whatever state this was, exactly. So what was this narrow-faced dude doing with a handgun? Aside from opening the chamber—which he couldn't figure out how to do at first—and sliding coppery rounds into the holes, one by one? It's possible that I barked at the sight, not a loud bark, just a low rumbly one, sending the message that Arthur was on the scene.

The man spun around in my direction, real fast, maybe the fastest human move I'd ever seen, almost as quick as a ca—oops. Let's not go there. Let's stay with the man, who was now pointing the gun straight at me. I didn't like that—didn't like it so much that I forgot to be scared.

"Stupid hound," he said, and lowered the gun.

Hound? Had he called me a hound? I'd heard I was a little of this and a little of that—my makeup being a subject that humans liked to discuss for some reason—but I'd never heard hound before. I decided then and there that I didn't like this dude, and I'm the type who likes just about every human I meet. Was this a good time for biting? Not a serious bite, more of a nip at the ankles? I was still making up my mind when the dude put on a jacket, stuck the gun deep in the front pocket, and said, "Let's go."

I was going somewhere with him? No way! I sat right down and found that even though I wasn't the slightest bit scared, I seemed to have backed out of the room and into the hall. The man came out, closed the door, and stepped around me. I didn't budge. Was I showing him a thing or two? You bet! No one messes with old Arthur. Actually I might not be that old, might have been a puppy fairly recently. I was born on a farm not far from here, and one day Bro came over for fresh eggs, and the rest is history, as humans say, which must mean there's no point in remembering all the details. That's my kind of history!

Meanwhile I was still plunked solidly on my butt in the hall, showing this gunslinger what was what. He reached the end of the hall and started down the stairs, disappearing from sight. It began to dawn on me that we had a problem. How could I show him what was what if he wasn't there to see it? I hurried down the stairs. By the way, you might hear—I'm not saying from whom—that old Arthur has a waddling sort of run. Don't you believe it!

THREE

QUEENIE

ARTHUR CAME WADDLING DOWN THE stairs. He was in a hurry, and when Arthur's in a hurry his waddling speeds up and gets wobbly, all parts of him going in different directions. Except for his stubby tail, which stands straight up. In short, not a thing of beauty. I watched this spectacle from my command post on top of the grandfather clock in the front hall. From there I have excellent sight lines to the front door, the front desk, the stairs, and the small parlor with its fireplace—unlit at the moment—and honor-system bar where guests like to grab drinks at the end of the day, and sometimes check the box beside their name on the list, and sometimes not. I keep track of things like that from my command post and have my ways of dealing with those not-so-good guests, which maybe we can get to later. As for guests, we seemed to have just the one, namely Mr. LeMaire, now sporting a heavy winter jacket and having some back-and-forth with Mom at the desk.

"Oh, we have tons of wonderful hiking," Mom said. She handed Mr. LeMaire a brochure. "What sort of hike were you looking for?"

Mr. LeMaire went through the brochure. "I'm interested in the old Sokoki Trail. And I don't see it."

Mom put on her glasses—she has the kind they call cat's eye, just another reason why Mom is Mom—and checked another copy of the brochure. "You're right," she said. "Probably because the old Sokoki Trail is not so easy to find. This one here"—she pointed at something else—"the Primrose, has quite similar terrain and is a snap to—"

"I am interested in the old Sokoki Trail," said Mr. LeMaire, "and only the old Sokoki Trail."

Mom took off her glasses and straightened up. I heard her foot beginning to tap. "Then I'd recommend a guide," she said.

"Very well," Mr. LeMaire said.

"I could try Matty Comeau," Mom said. "He's a cousin of mine, but that's not why I'm recommending him. Matty's the best guide in the valley. He's also an amateur archaeologist who probably knows more about—"

Mr. LeMaire made a backhanded waving motion, like he was sweeping something aside. "Fine. Can you make the arrangements?"

Mom got on the phone. I noticed that Arthur had positioned himself right behind Mr. LeMaire and seemed to be gazing at one of his ankles.

Mom talked on the phone for a bit and looked up. "Matty can't do today," she said. "How's tomorrow?"

"Today," said Mr. LeMaire. "Tell him I'll double his fee."

Mom is a very nice-looking person. Yes, no-nonsense, and her eyes can have a steely glint, but she still looks nice. Except for now, when a frown crossed her face unlike any I'd ever seen on her before.

"Matty?" she said, her voice level and kind of chilly. "The gentleman will double your fee."

Did I catch the sound of laughter on the other end of the phone? I thought so, but it was very faint.

Mom put down the phone, all of a sudden looking more cheerful and back to her pretty self. Did it have something to do with laughter? Human laughter is puzzling, but I'm pretty sure it's a good thing for them. "Today is out," she said.

"Out?" Mr. LeMaire's voice rose. "Not possible. Isn't there anyone else? It's not rocket science."

Ah. Rocket science. That comes up from time to time with humans. Last Fourth of July one of the guests turned out to be an actual rocket scientist. He showed Harmony and Bro how to build one. And what a sight it was when they lit the fuse! Why Arthur did what he did at that moment is something I'll never understand, but that's Arthur: in the end, a mystery. But the point was that rocket science leads to disaster. I was starting to be wary of Mr. LeMaire.

"Well," Mom said, "rocket science or not, I'm afraid that on such sort notice—"

"Mom?" said Bro. He was sitting in the chair beside the grandfather clock, meaning right below me—so I had a perfect view of his hair, with that strange stick-up thing at the back, like a clumpy feather—and was playing a game on his phone, a game where tiny humans were hacking at one another with swords.

Mom turned to him. He was looking at her even though his thumbs kept moving real fast and the tiny humans went on doing what they were doing. "Yes?" she said.

"I can do it," he said.

"Do what?"

"Take this, um, customer to the trailhead. For, like, double the usual fee."

"Well," Mom said, "I really don't think—"

"Hey, kid," said Mr. LeMaire, raising his voice over Mom's. "You know the way?"

Bro nodded. "Matty showed me. He's my cousin, and also the best hockey player who ever came out of this town, played for Dartmouth, and if he hadn't had all those concussions could have—"

"Skip the details. You get me there, I'll pay the fee."

"Uh, how much is it, Mom?" All this time, Bro's thumbs never stopped. That was kind of amazing! Did Bro have trouble in school? Was it possible he was a grade behind Harmony? I wasn't sure, might have slept through a conversation or two. But if running a whole battle of tiny humans without even looking had anything to do with school, then Bro should already have been in college.

"I believe Matty charges sixty-five dollars for a half day," Mom said.

"So double would be . . ." Bro's thumbs went still. "Like, um . . ."

"One hundred and thirty big ones," said Harmony, coming into the hall. "Count me in."

All eyes went to Harmony. Always a pleasure to see her. Harmony: the way she stood so straight; her glowing skin; and those big brown eyes, full of golden glints and every bit as sharp as Mom's. Yes, a thing of beauty. Although not quite in my class. I thought I'd point that out, just so you wouldn't get confused.

Mom nodded. "Good idea, Harmony."

"Whoa!" said Bro. "That means I have to split the fee?"

"Fifty-fifty," Harmony said.

"You two work it out," Mom said. "And why not take Arthur along? He could use the exercise."

"What's half of one thirty?" said Bro. Or something of that nature. My mind was on this latest development. Arthur was included in this shindig? And not me? Where was the justice in that? Look at him, still lurking behind Mr. LeMaire, his ugly snout down at ankle level, his head completely empty. In no time at all a certain someone could launch herself off the top of the grandfather clock and shake up that roly-poly world of his so it stayed shook up. But the better angels of my nature prevailed. There's a quiet dignity about me that I'm sure goes unnoticed by nobody. I glided down from my command post and made my silent way into the kitchen.

"Hi there, angel," Bertha said. How nice of her, but to the point, since I'd just been considering my angelic side. "You're late today. What kept you?"

Nothing important. Just the usual routine annoyance. Meanwhile Bertha poured fresh thick cream into a saucer and laid it at my feet. Bertha is a big fan. I'm her very favorite, as she's said so many times. But it never gets old. What a lovely woman! Everyone here at Blackberry Hill Inn was lovely, more or less, with one exception. Perhaps he'd get lost on this little hike, or whatever it was, never to return.

I licked up some cream in my delicate way. My manners are off the charts, unlike those of a certain piggish someone, and I'm not talking about the actual pig in our barn, who you may meet later. Or not. Meanwhile this cream, so fresh and sweet, was also off the charts. Didn't I deserve it? I'd had a pretty hard day so far, and it was still morning.

"That was quick," Bertha said. "Care for more?"

FOUR

ARTHUR

"YOU'RE TWINS?" MR. LEMAIRE SAID.

"Not the identical kind," said Bro.

Mr. LeMaire gave Bro a quick, eyebrows-raised sort of glance. Bro gets glances like that from time to time, I think when people realize he's got a lot going on upstairs. Are we alike in the upstairs department, me and Bro? I couldn't see why not. Out on our little hike with Mr. LeMaire, I tried to think of other strengths I had. When that didn't work, I tried not thinking about my other strengths, hoping that would work better. Another puzzle I had to deal with was that last remark of Mom's: *He could use the exercise.* What could she have meant by that?

Meanwhile we were on the main Mount Misty trail that starts in the woods behind Willard's General Store. It got colder right away, the kind of thing that often happens on Mount Misty. Cold doesn't bother me, not with my coat. I don't even feel it, except on my nose, which at that moment was picking up the gun oil scent coming from Mr. LeMaire's small backpack.

We rounded a bend and started up the first little rise, Bro in the lead, then Harmony and Mr. LeMaire side by side, and me last. Normally I go first, but how could I do that and keep an eye on Mr. LeMaire at the same time?

Harmony said, "Bro's actually older by four minutes."

"Uh-huh," said Mr. LeMaire.

"But guess what."

"I don't play guessing games."

Harmony's face clouded over just a bit. She dropped back a step or two. We kept walking till we came to the big rock at the first trail split, one of those rocks with lots of little sparkles in it. To one side, the trail stayed wide and easy; on the other side, it got narrow and much steeper. That was the side we took, the tall trees closing in around us and darkening the day. Mr. LeMaire began to huff and puff a bit. But not us. We were experienced hikers, me, Harmony, and Bro. And if I myself occasionally huffed or puffed, it was hardly ever and way beyond the reach of any human ears, which are mostly for decoration. Even if they're not all that great-looking. No offense, but human ears are so small! Check mine out sometime. Once a whole family of moths was living in one of them! Even though they weren't bothering me, the vet got rid of them.

Meanwhile Mr. LeMaire had stubbed his toe on a tree root and was saying some bad words.

"How about a little break?" Harmony said.

Mr. LeMaire turned to her. "I don't need a break," he said. But he leaned against a tree like someone who did need a break after all. Up ahead, Bro came to a stop, slowly leaning forward at the same time, like only his feet had stopped and the rest of him was still going. Bro often did funny things like that but no one seemed to notice. But hey! I did. Wow! Did I have it going on upstairs today or not? I even noticed that Bro's shoelaces were untied. And it didn't bother him at all, meaning he was a great hiker. He's a good hockey player, too, and so is Harmony. They're actually on the same team this year, the U-12 all-stars, but there have been problems, which maybe we'll get to later. And what was the other thing I was trying to remember? Uh-oh. Maybe it's easier to just let the past disappear. How can you beat the here and now?

"But," Mr. LeMaire was saying, "since maybe you need a break, I'll take advantage of the opportunity to play your little guessing game after all. Here's my guess—you and this twin brother of yours weren't even born on the same day."

Bro turned quickly. "Hey! You know about us?"

"Why would I know about you?" Mr. LeMaire said. "I simply used logic. Your sister here implied there was something unusual about your twinship and I went with the most obvious choice, one of you born close to midnight and the other just after." He shrugged.

"Wow!" said Bro. "You must be pretty smart, huh?"

"My IQ happens to be four standard deviations on the plus side," Mr. LeMaire said.

"What does that even mean?" said Bro.

"It means, Bro," said Harmony, "that he has a real high IQ."

"Wow!" Bro said again. "Um, Harm? What's ours?"

"Our what?" said Harmony.

"IQ."

"Why would we have the same IQ? How many times do we have to go over this?"

Bro kicked at a small stone. "Just one more."

Sometimes when Harmony and Bro aren't getting along, he says something that makes her laugh, just a short, sharp laugh, kind of like a . . . bark. Did that mean Harmony and I had something in common? Hey! Was it possible we had the same IQ, whatever IQ happened to be?

But I was losing my grip on what was going on. Harmony laughed that short, sharp laugh and said, "We're like any other brother and sister, Bro, except we were born together."

"Okay," Bro said. "Got it this time, for sure."

"What I don't get," Mr. LeMaire said, "is why everyone calls you Bro. It can't be your real name."

Harmony and Bro exchanged a look. They have certain looks they share that are like a kind of talk. This was one of them.

"I started it," Harmony said. "And it caught on."

"I like it," Bro said. "And it's a lot better than . . ."

"Than what?" said Mr. LeMaire.

Bro looked down at the ground. "Ringo."

"Your real name is Ringo?" Mr. LeMaire said. He laughed, one of those mean laughs I don't like to hear. I sidled over toward Mr. LeMaire, closing in on his ankles. "Your parents named you Harmony and Ringo?"

The kids didn't reply.

"I get it," Mr. LeMaire went on. "Your mother named one of you and your father the other, or some similarly stupid negotiation. Am I right?"

"I don't know about the stupid part," Harmony said. "But something like that. What's your first name?"

Mr. LeMaire looked down that big blade of a nose. "Mister, to you." He straightened up. "Lead on, Bro."

We climbed through the Mount Misty woods, higher and higher, our breath now showing in the air. Sometimes those breaths of ours rose up and joined together above us. There are interesting sights in life, but don't ask me if they mean anything. The trail, real narrow and rocky, slanted off to one side, then switched back. Water ran nearby—I could smell and hear it. I could also smell squirrel, fox, and bear, the bear smell not recent. That was a bonus: I'd had a few experiences with bears, none good. Also, I could smell . . . peanut butter? Yes, peanut butter for sure.

I followed the smell, which took me off the trail and into a small clearing with some blackened stones in the middle. There'd been a campfire here, maybe earlier today. I sniffed around it and under a charred stick found the remains of a sandwich, PB&J. How nice of whoever it was! I rejoined our little expedition.

"Arthur!" Harmony said. "What's in your mouth?"

Me? My mouth? Why, nothing. Or at least not much. And now—chomp chomp—nothing at all, for absolute sure.

She gave me a close look. "You be good."

I trotted beside her, good as good could be, like an obedience-school star. I'd been to obedience school—more than once—and really stood out from the crowd, as the teacher had told Mom when she came to collect me that last time. Would I be going back soon? I hoped so, although I kind of recalled Mom's surprise at that bill, too. And money was a bit of a problem these days. Poor Mom. I thought to myself, *snow! snow! snow!* And wouldn't you know it? Wafting down through bare branches above came a big fat flake, and then another! I was stunned. This was maybe the most important moment of my whole life. To make sure of my new powers, I changed my thinking slightly to, *sausages! sausages! sausages!* But no sausages wafted down from the sky, at least not right away.

"Why are you whining like that?" Harmony said.

Whining? That was me? Shameful, even if I wanted sausages so bad. I got a grip.

Harmony, Mr. LeMaire, and I stepped over a narrow stream that crossed the path—me actually stepping right through—and found Bro waiting up ahead. He was gazing at a huge tree stump that stood beside the trail, big puffball mushrooms growing on its flat top.

"I think this is the tricky part," he said.

Mr. LeMaire was huffing and puffing now, no doubt about it, his face all sweaty despite the cold. He'd opened his jacket and one side drooped a little: the gun side.

"What are you talking about?" he said, taking out his map, that old one where he'd marked a red circle.

"Where we leave the main trail," said Bro.

"That's not what it shows here," Mr. LeMaire said.

The kids went to look at Mr. LeMaire's map. Did he make a move to start folding it back up? I thought so, but they got there before he could.

"Cool map," Harmony said.

"What's cool about it?" said Bro.

"Well, it's hand drawn, for one thing. And so old and faded. Where did you get it, Mr. LeMaire?"

"That's not important." Mr. LeMaire jabbed at the map. "What's important is that it shows the Sokoki Trail running directly off the main trail after three series of three switchbacks about halfway up. We're halfway up, but the last three series were of two each. Meaning this is not the place."

"Don't know about that." Bro turned away from the map. "But this feels right."

"Based on what?"

"Huh?"

Mr. LeMaire's voice rose. "You can't just have an opinion. It has to be based on something."

Bro crossed his arms in front of his chest. "Matty told me."

"Some cousin of yours?"

"The best guide in the Green Mountains," Harmony said.

"He said stump with puffballs, hang a right," Bro said. "Stump with poison ivy, keep straight." He jerked his thumb down the trail. "We passed the poison ivy one a while back, so . . ."

"I didn't see any stump with poison ivy," Mr. LeMaire said. Bro tilted up his chin in this stubborn way he has and didn't say a word. "So now we're supposed to bushwhack?"

"Not for long."

"How long?"

"Not too long."

"What's with you? Why can't you just—?" Mr. LeMaire's hands closed into fists. I went over and stood beside the gun pocket.

30

Mom has a special, even tone she uses when things need calming down. Now I heard the same kind of tone from Harmony. "What about if Bro goes on ahead and we wait here to see what he finds out?" she said.

Mr. LeMaire thought about that. His eyes narrowed in a way that did nothing to improve his looks, in my opinion. "No," he said, his hands unclenching. "We'll go together."

"There's lots of good hikes around here," Harmony said. "What's so special about this Sokoki Trail?"

Mr. LeMaire tilted his head slightly, maybe trying to see Harmony in a new way. "Did I say it was special?"

"You just seem especially interested in it," Harmony said.

"Heh heh," said Bro.

Mr. LeMaire turned to him. "What's funny?"

"Um, actually I'm not sure," Bro said.

Mr. LeMaire shot Bro one of those human looks that say the other dude is hopeless. But there's nothing hopeless about Bro. So what was happening? I got the feeling I might be missing a thing or two. No problem! Life goes on!

The wind rose. We'd reached the part of the mountain where the needly trees that stay green all year were replacing the bare ones that lose their leaves, meaning the wind made strange, high sounds in those needles. No one else seemed to notice.

"Since you're curious," Mr. LeMaire said, "it just so happens I'm interested in the history of this region."

"Yeah?" said Harmony. "Are you a history professor or something like that?"

Mr. LeMaire shook his head. "This is more of a hobby."

"What's your real job?" Bro said.

"That's rude, Bro," said Harmony.

"I asked nicely."

"You're a curious pair," Mr. LeMaire said. "Just remember what curiosity did to the cat. To answer your question, I'm an investor. Now can we get going?"

We got going, but my mind was elsewhere, namely back at curiosity doing something to the cat. Something bad? That was my takeaway. How would that work, exactly? I wondered what curiosity was. And could there be a way to make a cat—no particular cat, just any old cat—curious? That would have to be the first step. I forced my mind to think its very hardest.

Meanwhile, had Bro already squeezed through a small space between the puffball stump and some thorny bushes, and was he leading us on a steep, somewhat muddy, and pathless climb through close-together, needly trees? Something like that. At the same time, the wind kept rising and snowflakes kept falling, no longer the soft, fluffy kind but the hard, stinging kind, although they didn't sting me, of course, except for my nose. There was lots of grunting from Mr. LeMaire, and that was before it got so steep we had to go down on all fours. I was way ahead of the game on that one! I moved into the lead. It was nice to see humans on all fours, although I couldn't explain why.

"How much"—huff—"farther?" Puff. That was Mr. LeMaire, now way behind the rest of us.

"Uh," said Bro.

"What does that mean? Try speaking English for—"

"Here we go," Bro said, and all of a sudden we were in a little clearing, me first, followed by Bro, then Harmony, and finally Mr. LeMaire. Had he fallen? He looked kind of muddy.

The little clearing ended in a rocky cliff, not quite as straight up and down as a wall, that rose to about the height of a man standing on another man's shoulders, which I'd seen once at the county fair, an outing that had ended up being a little too exciting. Some steps were cut into the rock on the lower part; up above there were rusted handholds all the way to the top.

Bro pointed. "The Sokoki Trail starts up there."

"You expect me to scale this cliff?" said Mr. LeMaire.

"It's not really a cliff." Bro started up and reached the top in no time.

"What do you see?" Mr. LeMaire said.

"The trailhead. Can't miss it."

Mr. LeMaire climbed up. He didn't make it look easy. At the top, he glanced around and nodded. "Okay, I see it. Won't be needing you kids anymore."

"Huh?" said Bro.

"But you hired us to—" Harmony began.

"Worried about your fee?" Mr. LeMaire took out a real big roll of bills, peeled some off. "Fifty, one hundred, ten, twenty, thirty." He handed the money to Bro. "See you later."

"Well, if you . . ."

Mr. LeMaire turned and walked out of my view. I heard his footsteps as they moved off, fainter and fainter and finally silent.

Bro came down, taking to the air for the last part. Harmony held out her hand. "I'll hang on to that."

"Why not me?"

"Start with Mom's birthday earrings last year."

"I don't know what happened. They were in my pocket."

"Exactly."

Bro handed over the cash. We headed for home, snow falling harder. After a while, Bro said, "Am I dumb?"

"I wouldn't say that."

"How come you're a grade ahead of me?"

"We've been through this. Mom—and Dad, actually—plus the school thought some extra . . . seasoning would do you good."

"No one asked for my opinion."

"You could hardly string two words together back then, if you recall."

We walked down through the Mount Misty woods, down always easier than up.

"Dad, too?" Bro said.

"What about him?"

"The me needing more seasoning thing."

Harmony gave him a long look, then nodded, just a little nod.

"I'm older than you," Bro said.

"Four minutes."

"But still."

The back of Willard's General Store appeared through a gap in the trees.

"How about hot chocolate?" Harmony said. "We can afford it."

And could we afford some treats? Possibly a chewy, or some of Willard's Homemade Doggy Biscuits, extra-large? Maybe a whole bag? I hoped so.

FIVE

QUEENIE

I AWOKE FROM A LOVELY DREAM. IT WAS
all about birds. You should have seen the looks on their
faces when—

Well, never mind. Humans can be surprisingly squea-
mish when it comes to certain—what shall we call them?
Action scenes? I adore action scenes myself, especially
when they're featuring me. My claws are sharp and my
teeth are even sharper. But at the same time, I'm so soft
and cuddly. A rare combination: You might call it a gift.

I found myself on Harmony's bed, just about my
favorite napping venue in the whole house. Our bedroom—
Harmony's and mine—is a lovely little room with pine
walls and a view that stretches all the way beyond the
meadows, across the highway to Mount Misty. If I wasn't
mistaken—and that's a safe bet—the kids had set off with
our guest in that direction. Set off without me? That happens. Most of the time I don't mind. And then there are
other times. I leaped over to Harmony's desk—more of a

flowing motion, really—and gazed through the window, seeing no one out there, just the colored dots of a car or two on the highway.

This seemed to be one of those other times, when I feel the need for a little company. I went down the back stairs and into the kitchen. Nothing happening and no Bertha, meaning she'd gone for the day. The Christmas tree was standing nice and straight in the Big Room, now with lights strung on the lower part, but there was no sign of Elrod. There was only Mom, busy with paperwork in the office. That paperwork was all about money problems: I could tell from her face. I slipped under the desk and rubbed myself against her ankle, making things all better. She didn't seem to notice. Had that ever happened before? We *were* in a bad way.

I don't like being in a bad way. Have you ever noticed how a little adventure sometimes changes the mood? I decided on an expedition to the basement, for no particular reason, although if mice are an interest of yours, the basement at the Blackberry Hill Inn should be on your bucket list. I'm not saying you're guaranteed to see one—although you would be for sure if a certain someone didn't take the trouble to venture down there from time to time. That certain someone would be me. Just pointing that out in case you're a little slow on the uptake. Don't take it personally, as humans like to say. Meaning take it . . . some other way, even though it is a criticism.

To get to the basement, you go past the kitchen to the back hall of the house. It's the oldest part, with a worn wood floor that makes my paw pads feel nice. At the end of the back hall is a somewhat crooked door. There are a few things that need fixing in the part of the inn that the guests don't see, and Mom has plans all drawn up, but first we need—well, you already know: money. But back to the crooked door, so crooked that even if it's closed, someone good at squeezing through small spaces can get through the gap underneath.

Someone like, yes, me. I squeezed through and started down the stairs. It was all dark and shadowy, which doesn't bother me at all. Humans see pretty well when there's lots of light, but take that away and they're practically blind. Supposing, for example, you were outside at night, say right out back, near the bird feeder, perhaps not with permission, strictly speaking, and anxious humans were peering through the windows, wondering where that cool cat could be—they wouldn't spot you! It took me so many times before I realized this very important fact was true. It changed my life. Well, just the nighttime part.

Our basement is very big, with lots of rooms. The furnace room's the biggest, but there's also the storeroom, the sporting gear room, the laundry room, the room for broken furniture—all of those in the newer part of the building. I'd learned long ago that on an expedition like this one, the older part of the basement, with its dirt floor, cobwebs, and strange rusted-out farm machinery from long ago, was a better hunting ground. Not that I was hunting anything, not really. I was simply passing the time, staying out of mischief, being a quiet little kitty cat.

But I can't be blamed for smelling things, can I? I do have a nose—an adorable little button nose, as Harmony always says, unlike the nose of you-know-who. All creatures have a smell, mice included. A mouse's smell is actually quite strong, especially for such a little critter. Not an unpleasant scent, and one part of it—not the main part, but always there—is the scent of fear. That's not a smell you pick up from me and my associates in kitty-cat world; nor, to be fair, do you detect it on Arthur or others of his ilk. A slow-witted ilk, but not given to fearfulness. Lucky Arthur, out in the world at that very moment. Why him and not me? Was everything upside down? I came very close to falling into a bad mood.

Except I didn't, on account of the fact that I'd come across mouse smell. The old part of the basement has only one small window, high up at ground level, the glass so dirty hardly any light gets through. Beneath that window is an old metal coal chute, going back to long-ago days. Elrod had explained the whole thing to Bro, and one of us had been paying attention. I followed my nose—an adorable little button, in case I forgot to mention it—around the old furnace, huge and shadowy, past a stack of wooden crates, and over to the coal chute. And who was scurrying desperately up that coal chute, headed for the window? Why, a mouse! A rather fattish mouse, my favorite kind. I leaped up onto the coal chute, not in any hurry. The mouse wasn't going anywhere, not with that window closed. I'm way ahead of you, my rodenty friend! Enjoy these last extra moments on—

But no! What was this? The little scamp! Somehow, when he reached the top of the chute, he kept going, right through the window and out? How was that possible? I hurried up the chute, dug my claws into the windowsill, and had a look. And what did I find? In one pane of the window, the glass had broken and fallen away, except for a narrow sharp strip at the top. Could I get through? I was sticking out an exploratory paw when I noticed movement in the meadow. Harmony and Bro were coming this way. Plus it seemed to be snowing. Oh, and also: Arthur. He was waddling very slowly, the way he does when all tuckered out. Arthur's the type that gets all tuckered out a little too easily, in my opinion. And then came a terrible sight. Harmony knelt, said something to Arthur—something gentle, far from "Bad Arthur!" or "What a lazy boy!"—and scooped him up. No! No! But yes. She scooped him up—even though you would have thought that the pudgy mutt was pretty much unscoopable—and carried him the rest of the way home. Carrying a dog? Aren't dogs supposed to be working creatures? Arthur should have been pulling the kids in a cart or a sled. Dog carts! Dog sleds! These things had names for a reason! I backed away from the window in shock.

Sometime later, we were in the Big Room, trimming the tree. Mom was sitting by the fire, mostly working on her laptop; Bro was picking the colored balls and snowmen and elves and igloos and bells and all the other ornaments out of boxes and handing them to Harmony, up on the ladder; Harmony was placing each decoration carefully on a branch; and me, up on the top shelf of the bookcase in the corner, keeping my opinions to myself. Plus Arthur, if you must know, sleeping on his side in front of the fireplace, his chest rising and falling in the most annoying way.

Mom glanced out the window. It was almost dark outside.

"I'm getting a little concerned," she said.

"Yeah?" said Bro. "What about?"

"Mr. LeMaire, of course," said Harmony. "What if he's lost?"

"Lost?" Bro said. "All he has to do is come down the same way he went up."

"It's not so easy," Mom said. "I wish you hadn't left him alone."

"He insisted," Harmony said.

"Yeah, insisted," said Bro. "He wasn't even going to come across with the cash unless we split."

"That didn't happen," said Harmony.

"Sure did."

"Did not."

Mom raised her hands. "Listen to the two of you." She rose. "His cell number is on the registration card. I'm going to call him."

"No service on Mount Misty," Harmony said.

"Maybe he's back down—warming up at Willard's, for example."

Harmony checked her phone. "Willard's closed ten minutes ago."

"I'll try anyway." Mom left the room, headed for the front desk.

"Did," Bro said.

"Did not," said Harmony. She lost her grip on a bright red ball. It fell to the floor and shattered in lots of pieces. "Now look what you made do."

"Me?"

"Why do you have to be so stubborn? You're worse than a mule." Harmony climbed down the ladder and started cleaning up all the little red pieces. I watched her—always enjoyable to watch humans at work, helps pass the time—but my mind was elsewhere, namely on Bro and mules. We had a mule living in the barn at one time, name of Muley, if I recall. Yes, Bro could be stubborn at times, but he was nowhere near Muley's class. Once Elrod had tried to get Muley to move from his stall to the next one over. What an amusing morning that turned out to be! And afternoon as well. I realized to my surprise that I missed Muley, if only just a little.

Mom came back into the room. "No answer," she said.

Bro shrugged. "You just come back the way you went up."

Mom and Harmony both shot Bro a look. It was the same look—in fact, Harmony and Mom appeared quite similar in every way at that moment. As for the look, it said, *What are we going to do with you?*

Mr. LeMaire did not appear, not before supper, or while we finished trimming the tree, or when bedtime rolled around. Mom tried B and Bs, motels, and other inns in the valley to see if Mr. LeMaire had checked in at any of them, but he hadn't.

"I'm calling the sheriff," she said.

"Sheriff Hunzinger?" said Harmony.

"Have we got some other sheriff?"

"No, Mom. But what do you expect him to do?"

"His job," Mom said. "Find Mr. LeMaire."

"Sheriff Hunzinger, Mom? At night? In the middle of a snowstorm? When we don't even know if Mr. LeMaire is missing?"

"Why not?"

"Because the sheriff's, like, not a hiker," Bro said.

"I hope you're not about to make disparaging remarks about a person's weight or age," Mom said.

"Depends what disparaging means," said Bro.

"And he doesn't have to go himself—he could send Deputy Carstairs."

"They're not back from Disney World," Harmony said.

It just so happens that I know the Carstairs family, Emma Carstairs being a friend of Harmony's. I've even paid a visit to their house, just the once. They turned out to have a pet gerbil living on the premises. What a strange idea!

"I'm not looking for reasons to do nothing," Mom said. She picked up the phone. Then came a long conversation with Sheriff Hunzinger. My ears turned themselves in Mom's direction and I heard the sheriff's deep, rumbly voice pretty well. He pointed out that it was a moonless night with snow falling, mentioned that the department's only working snowmobile was in fact not working but headed to the shop, and added that the county line crossed the old Sokoki Trail somewhere or other, so the whole issue—and he was confident this LeMaire fellow would turn up safe and sound in the morning, meaning there was no issue—might not even be in the sheriff's jurisdiction. Or something like that. My mind had actually wandered back to memories of the Carstairs's gerbil, Jerry, if I'd caught the name. Are gerbils somewhat reminiscent of mice? I went back and forth on that question, nice and relaxed amid the soft paperbacks, and gazing at the flames slowly shrinking in the fireplace.

Not much later, we called it a night, Mom leaving the outside lights on and the front door unlocked. I mostly sleep on our bed, mine and Harmony's. No one could complain about the comfort level, and best of all is the fact that Harmony is a deep sleeper, so deep she hardly ever notices when I ball myself up in her hair. She has the thickest, softest hair—a rat's nest, Mom calls it, but I've had more experience than Mom with rats' nests and she's flat-out wrong. Just thinking about Harmony's lovely hair makes me sleepy.

And I did sleep well that night, at least at first. But then the fact of the unlocked door began to bother me. Not that we get a lot of break-ins here in snow country, and of course if we had a proper watchdog it wouldn't have mattered at all. But we had Arthur. A proper watchdog would not be zonked out every night on Bro's bed, but would be up and at 'em, on patrol. I rose and went downstairs.

The house was not completely dark, instead had a reddish glow from the Christmas tree lights. I stood by the front door. It was tightly closed. I heard nothing except the wind outside, and perhaps the faint sound of Arthur snoring upstairs. What was his purpose around here again? Remind me.

Since I didn't feel sleepy, I decided to do some patrolling of my own, starting with the basement. Not my first nighttime basement visit. I like it down there at night, so quiet and shadowy. Lots of humans are afraid of the dark, Emma Carstairs for one, and Mom for two. In her case, it started around the time Dad left. But back to me. I'm not at all afraid of the dark. I'm part of it! One of the shadows! Yes, and the only shadow with a mind of her own. Right now that mind was thinking: *Hi, fat little mousy! Wanna come out to play?*

But while there was plenty of fat little mousy smell around, there was no fat little mousy. I even climbed to the top of the old coal chute to make sure. Through the dirty window, I saw a very faint light moving around on faraway Mount Misty. Blink, blink, blink—and gone.

SIX

ARTHUR

I AWOKE TO FIND I HAD THE PILLOW ALL to myself, Bro for some reason lying sideways on the bed in a position that didn't even look comfortable. I had no complaints, comfort-wise—in fact, no complaints at all! I stretched a nice big stretch and—

"Hey, cut it out," Bro said. Or something like that; hard to tell with his face so tangled in the sheets. Was he asleep? His eyes were closed and all crusty and he was drooling big-time, two for-sure signs of Bro sleeping. I was tempted to lick up that drool. What a crazy idea! Instead I got up, had another stretch, a real good one, head way down and butt way up, and set off for the kitchen. What a great day this was going to be! I just knew it.

Often I'm the first one downstairs in the morning. I like to give Bertha a big warm welcome. But today we had kind of a mob scene: Bertha at the stove, Mom drinking coffee at the table, and Harmony, walking in just ahead of me, in her jammies and rubbing her eyes. Also there was one other party, sipping cream from a bowl in the corner. I'm not even a fan of cream, but suddenly I had a strong desire to—

"Arthur!" Bertha said. "Don't even think about it!"

Me? But I wasn't even thinking! This was so unfair. I hardly ever think. Bertha had to know that.

"And get away from that bowl."

But I—Oops. I actually seemed to be surprisingly close to the cream bowl. When had that happened? I backed away, so fast that I might never have been near the bowl at all. Then came one of those golden-eyed gazes from this other party, the one with cream on her face. Which she licked up immediately, of course, in that oh-so-goody-goody tidy way of hers. I'm not a fan of that golden-eyed gaze, let's leave it at that.

I went over to Bertha and sat by her feet. She gave me a pat. That was a good start. At the moment, she was rustling up some eggs. What went with eggs? Bacon! Wow! How come my mind was so sharp today? I had no clue.

Meanwhile Harmony was saying, "Any news, Mom?"

"Why, yes, as a matter of fact," Mom said. "Good news. Mr. LeMaire texted me not twenty minutes ago. He's fine."

"Whew," said Harmony. "Where is he? When's he coming back?"

"Actually, he's not coming back," Mom said. "He's gone home to Montreal."

"But what about his things?" said Bertha. "Aren't they still in his room?"

"He's handling all that," Mom said, taking her phone from the pocket of her robe. "I'll read you the text. 'Sudden work emergency. Took the train back home. Friend will come for luggage. Many thanks. Pls keep deposit.'" Mom put the phone away. "He paid for two days."

"Well, then," Bertha said. "That's that. Anyone for bacon?"

Later that morning we had hockey practice. That meant this wasn't a school day, so it had to be the weekend or Christmas vacation, unless I was missing something. School days aren't my favorite, since Mrs. Sidney, the driver, doesn't let me on the school bus, something about "the rules." I'd followed the bus to the school once or twice—or maybe more—but guess what: The school had the same rules! What were the chances of that happening? And so every time, Mom had to come collect me from the hall monitor—who turned out to be Mrs. Sidney's sister!—and drive me home, always saying the same thing: "Arthur! Are you listening? Don't let this happen again!"

I listened my very best but it was hard, because all I could think was, *Mrs. Sidney's sister! Can you believe the luck?*

After breakfast, the kids packed up their hockey bags and we headed to the door. Then came a horrible surprise.

"No, Arthur," Harmony said. "You have to stay."

Stay? The meaning of that being . . . ? I got the feeling *stay* might be an important—what did humans call it? Suggestion, maybe? Something like that. Or was it—oh, no!—a command?

"Why can't he go?" Mom said.

"Because of the last time," Bro said.

"But the walk'll do him good," Mom said. "Give him one more chance. Just make sure he understands the boundaries. You have to tell him multiple times."

So was I going or not going? A certain golden-eyed being—up on the grandfather clock and far out of range—was watching this whole back and forth in her usual irritating way. But then Harmony opened the door and said, "Come on, Arthur. Just remember—you have to be good."

And I bolted outside. *I won! I won!* This was going to be great. All I had to do was to remember to be . . . something or other. It would come to me.

I like all sports, excepting basketball. The ball is simply too big and unmanageable, even if you soften it up a bit with your teeth. But nothing's perfect, as humans say. Except for life itself! Wow! What an amazing thought! I was at my very best.

50

The drawback in hockey is the ice, so slippery it's hard to run on, even for me with my four sturdy legs and grippy claws. But the wonderful thing about hockey is the puck—cold and hard, yes, but when you bite into it, that hardness gives a little bit, sending a blissful feeling up and down your teeth. Which was why on this sunny morning, with fresh snow sparkling on the ground and in the trees, I couldn't wait to get to the rink. The taste of puck!

"Hey, Arthur, slow down!"

"What's with him?"

"He's going to make a grab for the puck again, I just know it."

Were they talking about me? I considered the idea for what seemed like a long time and decided it was unlikely.

We have an outdoor rink in our little town—the name of which escapes me at the moment—in a park about halfway between the inn and the school. Our team's called the Tigers. I had no problem with that until the day Bro and I were watching the Discovery Channel and it hit me that tigers were actually giant cats. After that I had a big problem. Why couldn't Dogs be the team name? Go, Dogs, go! What's wrong with that? Plus hockey's a team sport and we're team players, me and my kind. Ever met a cat—one single cat—who was a team player?

Boards are a big thing in hockey. The puck often goes bouncing off the boards, and so do the players. I have a good view of what's going on if I get up on my hind legs and rest my front paws on top of the boards. I used to sit with the players on the players' bench, but that didn't work out, for reasons I never got clear.

Mr. Salming, our mailman, was the coach. He was a tall, broad-shouldered dude with eyes that looked the exact same color as the ice. Right now he had the kids in a circle around him and was giving them a pep talk. Mr. Salming's pep talks never lasted long. He was one of those humans who didn't say much. But in action, Mr. Salming could do things. Once he'd shown the kids his slapshot. CRACK! And the sound of that crack was still in the air when the puck went whizzing into the goal and ripped right through the netting at the back.

"Today we'll start with some three-on-twos," he said. "Any questions?"

Silence. Then Foster Mahovlich said, "No questions, Harmony?"

Harmony gave him a quick frowning look.

"Usually you got questions," Foster said. Foster was by far the biggest kid on the team. He even had a bit of a mustache.

"Foster," said Mr. Salming. "Any questions?"

"Yeah," said Foster. "How come Harmony got no questions?"

"That's your question?"

"Yeah."

Mr. Salming blew his whistle. "Two minutes."

Foster's eyebrows—the same color and thickness as his mustache—rose way up. "You're sending me to the penalty box in a practice?"

"Nothing wrong with your ears," Mr. Salming said. Really? Nothing wrong with ears that small? But I gave Mr. Salming a pass. I liked Mr. Salming and tried to be outside whenever he came by on his route. There are two kinds of mail carriers: the ones with treats in their pockets and the ones without. Mr. Salming was the first kind.

"But for what?" Foster said. "What's the penalty?"

"You got two minutes to figure it out."

Foster stomped over to the penalty box—not so easy in skates—took his seat, and slammed the door. Out on the ice, the kids started in on the three-on-two drill, Mr. Salming's favorite, meaning I'd seen it many times. First the first line skated against the first defense, then the second against the second, then . . . well, you get the idea, all the kids rotating through real fast and Mr. Salming blowing his whistle practically nonstop, which hurts my ears like you wouldn't believe. Did there have to be whistles in hockey? Once I'd even made a sort of play for that whistle of his, and for one brief shining moment I had it! And then not.

Harmony played center on the first line. The center's in the middle, between the wings. Humans may not be the fastest runners, but put them on skates and you're in for a surprise. And here's another surprise. Even though Harmony was one of the smaller players on the team, maybe the smallest, she was also one of the fastest. She came zooming down the ice, stickhandling the puck nice and easy, leading her two wingers down on the first defense, which was usually Bro and Foster, but right now was Bro and Bro's buddy Mort, the best computer hacker in town! He'd even been investigated by the FBI, whatever that might mean.

Back to the practice. Oops, not quite yet, because all of a sudden there was somebody standing right beside me, a short but real strong-looking guy. Hey! Our cousin Matty. He gave me a big smile—and Matty's got the biggest smile in town.

"A hockey fan, huh, Arthur?" he said.

Well, more like a puck fan, but close enough. He scratched between my ears, his fingers powerful but gentle at the same time. Ah. What a day I was having, and it was still early.

Meanwhile, out on the ice, the defense was skating backward. Yes! Bro can actually skate backward faster than Mort can skate forward. He won five bucks off of Mort proving that, but instead of the cash, Mort had done

Bro's math homework for the month. Hockey's a team sport, don't forget.

Harmony skated right toward Bro, faster and faster. And he went faster and faster, too, Harmony veering to the side. Bro reached for the puck with his stick, but just as he was about to knock it away, Harmony zipped a pass to one of her wingers, free and open right down the middle. The winger flicked the puck into the net.

"Got a head for the game, that girl," said Matty, real quiet, maybe to himself. A good thing, because I didn't get it at all: Didn't we all have heads? I hated to even think what my life would be like without one.

Mr. Salming blew the whistle. "Nice, Harmony. Hold, hold, hold, and don't panic. Mental plus the physical. Real nice." He skated over to Bro, put his arm on Bro's shoulder. "Can't overcommit, son."

"Huh?"

"Meaning hold the position. Don't let her lure you off."

"Just let her walk right in?"

"She can't—not if you hold your position. It's all about the angles. Eventually she'll have to come to you."

Bro thought about that. Hey! He was really thinking! Didn't see that every day. "Angles?" he said. "Is that geometry?"

"I suppose," said Mr. Salming.

"We haven't gotten to geometry yet, Coach."

Mr. Salming's eyes seemed a little less icy, just for a moment. "Then you'll be ahead of the game."

"Perfect," Matty said, again very softly. And then his phone beeped. He gave me a quick pat and hurried away, leaving only his smell, a lovely smell that reminded me of the forest after rain.

Whistle. Rotation. And again. By the whistle after that, Foster's penalty was over and he came storming out of the penalty box, taking over from Mort. Harmony wheeled around at center ice—her blades flashing over the tiger head painted under the face-off circle, always an annoying sight—and flew toward the blue line, wingers spaced out wide. Bro and Foster skated back, back, back, and this time Harmony veered toward Foster. He went toward her, the way Bro had done or even more so. Hey! Had he missed that whole hold-your-position thing? But unlike Bro, Foster didn't make a stab for the puck, just kept coming and coming. Almost without effort—so smooth on her skates!—Harmony lofted a pass toward her winger, totally open, and once again he put the puck in the net.

But what was this? Foster didn't seem to realize the play was over? He kept charging and charging—Harmony not even looking, eyes on her winger instead—then lowered his shoulder and barreled right into her, crushing her against the boards. I felt the vibration in my paws, and I was on the other side of the rink! Harmony crumpled to the ice.

Foster backed away, a little smile on his face. I told myself, *Arthur, don't ever forget that little smile.* Meanwhile Bro came rushing toward his sister, ice chips flying off his skate blades. But Mr. Salming got there first. Harmony was already struggling upright. Her helmet with its face guard had been knocked clear off her head. Her face was very pale. I scrambled over the boards, and . . .

But no. I ended up losing my grip and tumbling backward into the snow. Was that called a somersault? I thought so. My very first one, although this wasn't the time. I was so mad! Next thing I knew I was somehow over the boards and inside the rink, trying to run but mostly skidding my way toward Harmony.

"Foster, what in god's name?" Mr. Salming was saying. "You know there's no bodychecking in this league. What were you thinking?"

"Well, Coach," said Foster, still with that little smile on his face, "there's checking next year. I was just helping Harmony get ready. Maybe she won't be so big on hockey when there's checking."

The expression on Mr. Salming's face changed. Now he was angry, too, just like me. Was he planning on biting Foster? I sure was.

"Wrong answer," Mr. Salming said.

Foster shrugged. "Best I can do, Coach."

That was when Bro, who'd been standing by Harmony, his hand on her arm, skated over, stopping right in front of Foster. Bro wasn't much taller than Harmony, but he was quite a bit broader; still, nowhere near Foster's size. He took off his helmet, dropped it on the ice, and looked Foster right in the eye.

"You're a dirty player," he said. That weird clump of hair on his head was sticking straight up. Bro gave Foster this level-eyed look you saw from him sometimes— actually when he was at his best, in my opinion. And who knows Bro better than me? "I don't like dirty players," he said.

"No?" said Foster. He, too, dropped his helmet and stared down at Bro, but not in a level-eyed way, more like hateful. "Wanna do something about it?"

This was where you might think the coach would step in, but Mr. Salming did not. He just let it happen, and what happened was Bro rearing back and punching Foster bang on the nose. There was a cracking sound, not loud, more like when Elrod breaks a stick in two for kindling, and then blood came gushing from Foster's nose.

He clutched his nose, screamed, "Oh my god! Blood!" And went down on one knee. Mr. Salming nodded, that little human nod that means everything's shipshape, although what we had going on at the rink didn't seem shipshape to me. I did notice that I'd lost the urge for biting.

Mr. Salming blew his whistle. "Practice is over. Next game's Thursday, nine a.m. Be here eight thirty sharp." He tossed Foster a towel.

We walked home, me, Harmony, and Bro. They had their hockey bags slung over their shoulders. I was carrying something, too, in my mouth of course, which is how I do my carrying. It was just a little round black something that had been lying on the ice, unnoticed in all the confusion.

"You okay?" Bro said.

"Don't want to talk about it," said Harmony.

"Uh-huh," said Bro. "But are you, like, fine?"

"I said I didn't want to talk about it. And I'm mad at you."

"Mad at me?"

"I can fight my own battles."

"Huh?"

Harmony turned on him. "You're saying I can't?"

"No, I'm just—"

"'Cause he knocked me on my butt?"

"No," Bro said. "You, uh, can do that—fight your own, whatever it was. I only—"

Harmony whipped the hockey bag off her shoulder and thrust it at him. "Take this home. I'm going for a walk."

"A walk. Where? I'll go with you. We could get hot choc—"

"I'm going by myself."

Harmony turned on her heel and walked away. Bro and I exchanged a look. "What did I do?" he said.

Popped Foster a good one! That was my takeaway on the whole morning so far. A morning with a happy ending, in my book. So why was I the only happy one?

Bro hoisted Harmony's bag on his free shoulder and headed for home.

"Come on, Arthur," Harmony said.

And even though I did feel like being at home, possibly lounging by the fire, I trotted off after Harmony. Why? I had no idea.

We walked side by side, me and Harmony, the main sound being the crunch crunch of her boots on the snow. Some of the time she was crying, but soundlessly. Tears came rolling out of her eyes, down her face, and falling into the snow. I trotted ahead, turned, and showed her the puck, hoping to distract her. At first she didn't notice, but later— after I'd bumped against her legs once or twice or maybe more—she did. She gazed down at me and smiled. Smiling through tears? Was that an expression? It was what I saw now. I loved Harmony, no doubt about that. She knelt and gave me a nice pat. I dropped the puck and licked her face.

"I like hockey, Arthur." She rose and put the puck in her jacket pocket. "I'm going to play."

Sure. Why not? I didn't see any problem.

Not long after that, we were enjoying hot chocolate at Willard's. More accurately at a picnic table on the deck behind Willard's, due to some incident that may or may not have occurred inside on a previous visit. The hot chocolate was for Harmony, of course. I had a nice bowl of fresh water, my go-to drink. It was sunny on the deck, maybe on the cool side, but the air was still, the tree branches on the lower slopes of Mount Misty motionless, the snowy summit shining gold. Did we have a single care in the world? Not me!

Harmony gazed at Mount Misty over the rim of her mug. Hey! She was rocking a chocolate mustache! Licking it off struck me as a very good idea. I moved a little closer. Good things can happen in life, but you have to be ready.

"You know what I still don't understand, Arthur?"

Why we hadn't ordered a side of Willard's Famous Home-cured Bacon? That was my only thought.

"What's the big deal with the old Sokoki Trail in the first place? That's what I don't get."

The old Sokoki Trail? That sounded familiar.

"Mr. LeMaire never said. I wonder if he left tracks in the snow. It might be interesting to . . ." She didn't finish that thought, not out loud. Was the finishing part . . . *order up some bacon?* I waited to see. But no bacon got ordered. Instead Harmony rose and—oh, no—licked off her chocolate mustache. "Plus I . . . I just don't want to go home yet. And a walk will do us good."

It would? I was plenty good just like I was. Why mess around when—

"Arthur? You're lying on your back? Get up. Let's roll!"

Why were people always saying that a walk would do me good? I liked walking—up to a point—but I also liked other things, bacon for example. How come no one ever said, "Care for some bacon, Arthur, my friend? Bacon'll do you good"?

Various thoughts—but pretty much all of them about bacon—occupied my mind as we followed the trail we'd walked yesterday, up and around the side of Mount Misty. The snow wasn't deep—hardly any at all under the trees— and we zoomed along, the way you do when your mind is elsewhere. Harmony didn't say a word the whole time, not until we reached the cliff at the base of the old Sokoki Trail. She gazed up.

"Bodychecking starts next year, Arthur," she said. Then, after a long pause, she added, "I love hockey."

I gazed up at her. She was so lovely! I sat down right on her foot, just letting her know we were good for always. As for what she was talking about, I couldn't tell you.

Harmony gave me a quick pat, took a deep breath, and—wow!—gave herself a little shake. Just when you think she can't get any better, she does.

"Okeydoke, Arthur. Think you can scramble up? It's not that steep."

What was this? She wanted me to scramble up this sheer cliff?

"Come on. You've got four feet."

Maybe so. But what difference did that make?

Harmony unzipped her jacket, reached into an inside pocket, took out a biscuit. To be precise, a Willard's Homemade Doggy Biscuit, extra-large. Not long after that, we found ourselves on top of the cliff, which had turned out to be not so steep after all, practically level ground. We had a quick little picnic—energy bar for Harmony, biscuit for me—and set off on the old Sokoki Trail.

SEVEN

QUEENIE

MOM WAS PUTTING UP DECORA-
tions around the front desk: paper bells,
silver icicles, Santa dolls. There's constant
entertainment here at the Blackberry Hill Inn, especially
if you're the quiet, watchful kind, and I am. Me: many,
many things, of which quiet and watchful aren't close to
the most amazing, but they're part of the package.

I love watching Mom—or any humans—at work. They
get so focused. It's kind of cute, really. Because when all
is said and done, what difference . . . but enough of that! It
was Christmas. The mood should be bright at Christmas.
I stretched out on the grandfather clock, my heart full of
nice feelings for all my fellow creatures. With one exception, as I'm sure you understand by now.

Mom started to hang a wreath on the wall behind the
desk. To make space, she moved a mirror onto a different
hook. And lo and behold! What suddenly appeared in that
mirror, up near the top? Why, the image of a stunning,

golden-eyed individual, relaxing in the most elegant fashion on top of an old grandfather clock. Here was entertainment of the very highest quality. The individual slowly raised her glorious tail, and curled and uncurled it in the most languorous way, for no reason other than the sake of beauty. For a moment I turned my gaze to Mom and sent her a strong, simple message. *Mom? You won't ever be shifting that mirror again, will you?*

Perhaps Mom didn't get the message, distracted by the entrance of Bro, carrying two hockey bags. He closed the door. And Harmony was where, exactly?

"Hi," Mom said. "How was practice?"

"Good."

She looked past him. "Where's Harmony?"

I was no longer surprised that Mom and I often thought along similar lines. It has been clear to me for some time that we have a lot in common, although golden eyes are mine alone. When it comes to looks, there's no missing the big gap between me and, well, everyone. Fair is fair.

"Uh, Harmony?" Bro said.

"Your sister. The one you go to hockey practice with."

"She went for a walk."

"A walk? After all that exercise?"

"With Arthur."

Mom nodded like that made sense. Arthur could always use a walk, although all those walks of his never seemed to produce the slightest result.

"What's for lunch?" Bro said.

"Whatever you make yourself," Mom said. "Just don't blow up the kitchen. And first run upstairs and bring down Mr. LeMaire's bag."

"Huh? How come?"

"So we'll have it handy by the desk when whoever he sends comes calling for it. Plus we'll free up the room. Do I need any more reasons?"

Bro thought that over. Then he smiled. Bro has a very nice smile, actually not as broad as Harmony's, and even kind of shy. "That's a joke, right?"

"Partly," said Mom. She handed him a key. Bro started up the wide staircase that led to the guest rooms. I hadn't been up there in some time. So why not now? I took one last lingering look in the mirror and leaped down from the grandfather clock, if leaping was the right word for such a silent, fluid movement.

"Hey, Queenie," Bro said. "How'd you get in here?"

Bro was looking at me—perched on the desk in the big guest room at the end of the hall—with surprise. He really hadn't noticed me following him the whole way, and entering the room side by side? Was Bro even safe out in the world on his lonesome? Did I have to keep an eye on him?

A suitcase lay open on the bed. Bro moved closer to gaze inside. I could see perfectly from where I was: neatly folded clothing; Dopp kit; sneakers; phone charger; and a postcard. An old postcard: I could smell its mustiness. Bro picked it up.

"Hey," he said. The front of the postcard was a picture of a man standing by a truck. " 'Foster Mahovlich Transport, Anything and Everywhere, established 1919,' " Bro read aloud. He turned it over. "It's addressed to LeMaire and Company, in Montreal, October 12, 1932. There's no signature and no message, except this one letter, *C*." Bro said "Hmm" a couple of times, then slipped the postcard into his pocket and closed the suitcase. "Come on, Queenie, you can't stay here."

I hadn't been planning to, but now that it was forbidden, I reconsidered. At the same time, I was suddenly in a curious mood. Oh, I know what you're thinking. Don't you believe that old saying about curiosity. We in the cat world are not so easy to get rid of. And who in their right mind would even want to get rid of us? I thought about that as I glided down the stairs beside Bro. The problem was that a surprising number of humans were not in their right minds, at least not all the time. But only my opinion. Don't get upset. Getting upset too easily is a sign of not being in your right mind, by the way. Just sayin'. No offense. But you know who you are.

Bro wheeled the suitcase over to the front desk.

"Thanks," said Mom. She glanced at the door. "Sure practice was okay?"

"Uh-huh. I found kind of a cool thing up there."

"Oh?"

He laid the postcard on the desk. Mom put on her cat's-eye glasses. For a moment she looked a little like me. Not close to the full effect, of course. But still. Mom had a bit of cat in her, not something you see every day. Finding dog in just about every single human? Easy peasy.

Mom examined the postcard, front and back.

"Any relation to the Foster Mahovlich on our team, Mom?" Bro said.

Mom nodded. "Great-grandfather, I would say, or even great-great-grandfather. He was the one who made all the money."

"How?"

Mom tapped the postcard with her fingernail. "He started this trucking company, long gone now, hauling logs to the mills, I think it was, and maybe lumber down to Boston and New York. After that came all the real estate."

"How rich are they?"

"More than rich enough. I don't know the details, but they own thousands of acres in this part of the state, including Big Snow Ski Resort."

"Yeah?" said Bro. "I didn't know—"

The front door banged open and a large man came in, one of those types with a barrel of an upper body and sticklike legs. He looked red-faced and angry, in fact, pushing a sort of invisible anger wave ahead of him. I could feel it.

He stabbed his thick finger at Bro. "There he is!" he said. "And don't give me that innocent look, you sneaky little—"

Mom interrupted. "Mr. Mahovlich? Is there some problem?"

Mr. Mahovlich's voice rose. "Is there some problem? I've just come from the hospital and you bet there's a problem. This sneaky little b—sneaky little sneak of yours busted my son's nose. Took the doc fifteen minutes to stop the bleeding. Like a stuck pig!" Mr. Mahovlich came forward, now wagging that thick finger at Mom. "You gonna let him get away with it? And be careful with your answer. I can loop in my lawyers in a heartbeat."

Mom tilted up her chin. I love that look. It's a family thing: Harmony and Bro do it, too. We don't like being pushed around in this family.

"I don't know what you're talking about, Mr. Mahovlich. And I'd appreciate it if you'd—"

"I'll tell you what I'm talking about! This sucker-punching offspring of yours—"

Bro's face went bright red, even redder than Mr. Mahovlich's. "It wasn't a sucker punch! We dropped our helmets and—"

"Whoa!" said Mom, raising both hands like stop signs. "Was there some problem at practice?"

"That's one way to put it," said Mr. Mahovlich.

"He started it," said Bro.

"What a load of—"

"WHOA!" Mom said.

That *whoa* shook the house. I wouldn't have thought Mom capable of a *whoa* like that.

"One at a time. You first, Mr. Mahovlich. And please, let's all try to calm down."

"I'll calm down after you assure me that this hooligan will be punished—and punished severely."

"For what?"

Mr. Mahovlich banged his fist on the desk. He wore a huge golden watch, a beautiful watch, I suppose, matching the color of my eyes. But that wasn't enough to make me like him.

"For what? I've been trying to tell you. He flat out—" Mr. Mahovlich raised his fist, intent on banging the desk again, but now he noticed the postcard, lying right there. He froze. "What's this?"

Mom glanced down. "A postcard."

Mr. Mahovlich tried to snatch it up, but Mom can be quick—not cat-quick, of course, but surprisingly close. She laid her hand on the postcard.

"Not just any postcard," Mr. Mahovlich said. "Where did you get it?"

Mom turned to Bro. "I was just finding that out."

"Um," said Bro. Then he added "uh," followed by another "um." He shifted around—and suddenly spotted me! A very nice sight, of course, and it seemed to have a calming effect. Bro straightened up and said, "A guest left it behind."

"Who?" said Mr. Mahovlich. "What guest?"

"We have strict confidentiality rules when it comes to our guests," Mom said.

"Huh? What does that mean?"

"It means we don't blab about them."

Mr. Mahovlich clenched his teeth, making his jaw muscles bulge in a most unpleasant way. He jabbed a finger at the postcard. "I want it," he said.

"It's not yours." Mom's hand moved a little, now covering the postcard completely.

"But it's . . . it's a family memento," Mr. Mahovlich said. "I'll pay you. How does one hundred dollars sound?"

Mom did not reply, just gave Mr. Mahovlich a steady look.

"Two? Three?"

Three hundred dollars? For a crummy old postcard? Sounded good to me. Mom? The money? We have no guests at the moment? Hello?

"It will be returned to the owner." Mom put the postcard in a drawer. "Like any other forgotten item. Now, where were we, Mr. Mahovlich?"

Mr. Mahovlich's eyes stayed on that drawer for what seemed like a long time. Then he made a big show of checking his watch. Because he wanted us to see how beautiful it was? Did he care what we thought about anything? Mr. Mahovlich shot Mom an unfriendly look and Bro an even less friendly one. "To be continued," he said. He backed up a step or two, wheeled around, and strode out of the inn, slamming the door behind him.

Mom turned slowly to Bro. "All right, mister—the truth about hockey practice, the whole truth, and nothing but."

EIGHT

ARTHUR

DO YOU KNOW ABOUT THE OLD SOKOKI Trail, Arthur?"

I did not. But I did know that me and Harmony were hiking on it, so maybe everything would soon be clear. Hey! What was with me? I was getting brainier and brainier with every passing day! In fact, maybe this was enough braininess. I got the feeling too much braininess might be tiring. And wasn't it time for a little rest, possibly accompanied by a snack of some sort? Nothing elaborate. Just scraps—a leftover sandwich crust or a rolled-up baloney slice—would do. I glanced over at Harmony—moving a little on the rapid side—to see if a snack might be in the plans.

She looked at me. "Everybody's wrong about you, aren't they, Arthur? You're not a complete blank in there, I can tell."

Of course I wasn't a complete blank! What a strange idea! That was my only thought at the moment. But a great one! Otherwise my mind was nice and empty.

We kept moving. This trail—I was pretty sure it had a name and it would come to me eventually—was real easy to follow, since somebody had been by already, somebody in snowshoes, packing down last night's snow, really not that deep to begin with. We went up and up and then it got flat, headed sideways across Mount Misty. The air was so still among the trees—most all of them of the Christmas-tree type—and there was nothing to hear but the crunch of Harmony's boots on the snow, I myself moving silently, and if not silently, at least pretty quietly. If I tried hard I could also hear the beating of my heart, thump thump, thump thump, nice and steady, always there when I needed it. And even when I didn't! Who's luckier than me?

"Matty says the old Sokoki Trail goes way back to Colonial days, or even earlier," Harmony said, interrupting my thoughts at just the right moment. "He's got the mountains in his blood."

Sokoki! I knew it would come to me. But mountains in his blood? That sounded terrible. Poor Matty! And he was one of my favorite humans, the best guide in the mountains, which was why we always recommended him to our guests, not to mention what a fine head-scratcher he was. I made what Mom calls a mental note to give Matty a nice big kiss the next time I saw him.

"Do you think Mr. LeMaire had snowshoes?" Harmony said. "I don't remember seeing any."

Neither did I. Pretty much all I remembered of him was that gun in his jacket pocket.

"Arthur? What are you growling about?"

Me? I listened. Yes, my growl for sure, low and rumbly. Grrr. Grrr. The party on the other end of that growl must have been shaking in his boots. I wondered who it could be.

"Cut it out."

I cut it out.

We crossed a frozen stream, the ice black and mostly clear of snow, except for a few wisps here and there.

"Hey!" Harmony said on the other side. "No more snow-shoe prints."

I hadn't spotted that little detail. But now that she mentioned it, I saw no prints, no prints for sure. We were a great team, me and Harmony. She peered up and down the stream.

"Whoever it was must have left the trail."

Wow! Was Harmony cooking or what?

"I wonder whether we should follow the stream." She turned toward the woods, where the trail led into the trees and vanished from sight. "But that's clearly the trail, and the trail's what Mr. LeMaire was interested in. Let's roll, Arthur."

Or, if this was getting too complicated—and that was my take—we could head for home, curl up in front of a nice fire, just hang for a while. Anything wrong with that?

Harmony was real big on rolling, except we never rolled anywhere, always stayed on our feet. Although there was the one time last summer when she took me on her bike. That hadn't ended well, on account of—

"Arthur?"

Did I detect a sort of extra firmness in Harmony's voice? Not harsh or angry: nothing like that ever came my way from Harmony. But firmness? Yes, I felt it. We rolled.

Although we were rolling, side by side in a nice, companionable way, hardly bumping into each other at all—"For god's sake, Arthur!"—it couldn't be said that we were rolling fast. The trail soon got much too steep for speed, winding up and up through trees so thick it was almost dark down below. Plus the trail itself was now very hard to pick out. But Harmony seemed to have no problem, just strode ahead, not panting at all. In fact, there was hardly any panting going on from anybody! We were pros at hiking, Harmony and me.

She slowed down when a little tower of stones appeared. "Good thing someone blazed the trail, Arthur. Otherwise we'd be lost."

What was this? Someone had built the little tower? Had we passed others kind of like it? I searched my mind, had faint memories of that. I had much stronger memories of Bertha's sausage as it came spinning through the air. That memory grew bigger and bigger until there was no room for others.

Soon we came to a small frozen waterfall, a strange and beautiful sight.

"Arthur! Don't lick that. You'll get your tongue stuck."

Uh-oh. Was I licking at the bottom of the frozen waterfall? Maybe. But my tongue didn't get stuck. Instead I lapped up icy drops of water. Delicious! Maybe the best water I'd ever tasted. I promised myself to come back here often—which I changed to never the moment it hit me that getting to this lovely water was such a huge production. There's something to be said for the water in my kitchen bowl at home, even when it's stale and has a dead fly or two floating on the surface.

I was still thinking about those flies—funny how the mind works!—as we left the frozen waterfall behind, worked our way across a steep ridge, and suddenly found ourselves on much flatter ground, like a tiny, snowy meadow, with a strange tangle of branches and a fallen tree or two on the other side, like a sort of roof over a hidden, shadowy space.

Harmony came to a stop. "What a beautiful place! And so quiet. Can you hear anything, Arthur?"

Where to start? With the plane flying high above, beyond the clouds? Or the squirrel scurrying through the woods? What about a clump of snow plopping down from—But

I left my little list right there, distracted by a smell that meant something to me, although I couldn't think what. Not a strong smell, like when Bertha opens the oven and pulls out a roast beef, for example. This was much weaker, but I had no trouble identifying it: the smell of human earwax of the male kind. That smell seemed important to me, although I couldn't have explained why. I followed it over to the side and into the woods.

"Arthur? What are you doing?"

Following earwax smell, that's what. It seemed like the most important thing in the world. My tail was going real fast, totally out of control. No time at that moment to remember how to slow it down. I rounded a spiky bush, the earwax smell getting stronger, and sort of trapped under the spikiest part, almost totally hidden, I found something.

A sheet of paper? Paper that was quite thick and bigger than the normal paper you see, when Mom's doing the bills, for example. This particular paper reminded me of something, something like a . . . map. A map? A map! And not just any map, but the map I'd first seen in Mr. LeMaire's room, when he was putting a red circle on it. And sure enough, I spotted a red circle, over toward one edge of the map. Wasn't this Mr. LeMaire's map? Weren't we searching for Mr. LeMaire? I started to get pretty excited! Me, Arthur! What a good good boy! I could almost hear Harmony saying that. No almost! I could hear them all—Harmony, Bro, Mom, Elrod, Bertha, Mr. Salming, even Foster Mahovlich—all of them lined up and cheering their heads off! *Arthur! Arthur! What a good good boy!*

Meanwhile I had just about freed the map—what was left of it—from under the bush. And soon I'd be laying it at Harmony's feet. I trotted back to the clearing, the map in my mouth. I couldn't help noticing that this particular map turned out to be tasty. Chewing on paper can be surprisingly pleasant, in case you didn't know that already. It gets wetter and slobbier the more you chew it and then all at once you realize it's gone! Wow! I entered the clearing and raced toward Harmony, head down, ears straight back in the breeze.

"Arthur?"

Yes, it was me, Arthur, coming to save the day! In fact, coming so fast that my paws lost their grip and I actually ended up . . . rolling! Harmony had said *roll* and here I was rolling right up to her and laying a wonderful trophy at her feet.

"What have you got there?"

Harmony squatted down and picked up a small sort of whitish blob. Her eyes narrowed. "Is this some kind of . . . ?"

She took off her mittens and tried to spread out the blob and make it flat. That didn't turn out to be so easy, the flattened-out blob kind of shredding itself in a wet way and somehow shrinking in her hands.

Harmony squinted at what was left of the thing. "Is that a red circle? Don't tell me this is the . . . ?" Yes! A circle! I was right. Was this the best moment of my life or what? Harmony tried to smooth out the red circle part, her fingers moving so carefully and her tongue sticking out a bit, which meant this was as careful as a human could be. But! Oh, no! Nothingness! The whole soggy mess, red circle and all, just sort of slid off her hands, came apart, and vanished, leaving not a trace in the snow. Harmony peered down, laid her hand on the snow—a beautiful hand, by the way, squarish and strong. Her face darkened. Then, slowly, she looked up at me. Her face was still dark but her voice was gentle.

"Good boy," she said, taking a long, slow breath, maybe the kind called a sigh. "You done good."

Yes! Yes! Yes!

"Hey! Cool it!"

Cool what? Licking Harmony's face? Nothing else came to mind. I ramped it down. But I'd done good! You don't forget things like that.

Harmony rose. "Now show me where you found it, Arthur."

Right! No problem. I trotted away, made a turn, then another, and another, and another, round and round the clearing, and—

80

"Arthur! You're going in circles!"

Whoa! That couldn't be good. I came to a stop—and just in time, since all this trotting had a tiring effect.

"The map, Arthur. Where did you find it?"

The map? I remembered the map, but the truth was I'd forgotten where I'd found it. I sniffed the air, always a good move at a time like this. And then came a surprising scent. Not the human earwax smell, although I picked up traces of it. But there was another smell mixed in, much stronger, the kind that gets your attention: the smell of bear.

"Arthur? You're pointing all of a sudden? You know how to point?"

I didn't understand the question. I just kept on doing what I was doing, standing still with one of my front paws raised and my nose in the air. After not too long, my nose—which is actually very smart—figured out where the bear smell was coming from, namely that shadowy space under the roof of the fallen trees and branches. I headed that way.

Harmony followed me across the clearing. When we got close, she said, "Arthur! That could be a lair!"

Lair? A new one on me.

"Where a bear hibernates for the winter—and they don't like to be disturbed. Stop!"

And maybe I would have, but now there was another new smell, mixed in with bear and earwax. This something new made all the hairs on the neck of my thick coat rise up. I kept going, right up to this sort of hole or cave or whatever it was, and poked my head inside. It was too dark to see very well, but my nose already knew. I barked, a high-pitched sort of bark that didn't even sound like me.

"Arthur?"

Then Harmony was crouching beside me. We peered into the dark space. Way at the back, someone seemed to be lying down. This someone was not bear-sized or bear-shaped, but my nose already knew all that, even knew who this was.

"It's not a bear, is it?" said Harmony, her voice very quiet and also a bit shaky.

I didn't like hearing that shakiness from Harmony. It was time for old Arthur to step up. I moved forward. Harmony followed.

"It's a man," she whispered. And when we got closer: "It's . . . it's Mr. LeMaire!"

We got down in front of him. He lay on his back.

"Mr. LeMaire? Are you asleep?"

But his eyes were open.

Harmony put her hand on his shoulder, gave it a little squeeze. "Mr. LeMaire."

He did not move, or reply, or do anything. Harmony reached up and shifted some branches. A narrow beam of light shone through from above, falling on Mr. LeMaire's still and waxy face. Harmony lowered her own face very close to his, almost touching his nose.

"He's not breathing, Arthur."

Well, I knew that.

"But I don't see anything that—" Very gently, she got her hands under him and tried to roll him onto his side. That didn't turn out to be so easy. At last she got him shifted a little bit. His head flopped forward and we saw the back of it.

"Oh, no."

Harmony let him go and shrank back real fast. The back of Mr. LeMaire's head was all bashed in. The next thing we knew we were out of that horrible dark space, back in the clearing and breathing nice fresh air. Harmony's face was as white as the snow. I could hear her heart beating, way way too fast.

"No bear did that, Arthur. Did he fall? But if he fell, then how did he get into that place?" Then with no warning, she leaned forward and puked. Poor Harmony! Puking's no big deal for me and my kind, but I know it's different for humans. I stood beside her, wondering whether licking up the puke would be a good move.

When the puking was all over, Harmony straightened up, hands on her hips, taking deep breaths. That was when a short but powerfully built man stepped out of the woods on the other side of the clearing, snowshoes on his feet and an ax over his shoulder. It was Matty! Always nice to see him. Especially now. He looked at us in surprise.

"Harmony?" he said.

"Matty? What . . . what are you doing here?"

"Clearing trails after the storm," Matty said. He gave Harmony a close look. "And you?"

"Oh, Matty—something terrible has happened."

NINE

QUEENIE

S O MR. MAHOVLICH WAS TELLING THE
truth?" Mom said. "You really broke Foster's nose?"

"But, Mom!" Bro said. "He tried to hurt her!
There's no bodychecking till next year."

Mom held up her hand. This discussion of hockey practice had been going on and on. I don't care for hockey or
any other sport. Sports all involve human movement, which
I don't find all that graceful, certainly not in comparison
with other creatures I could name. But back to the front
hall, with Mom behind the desk, Bro sitting in the rocker
near the grandfather clock, and me on my command post
up on top.

"I don't want to hear that word ever again," Mom said.

"What word?" said Bro.

"Bodychecking."

"How come?"

"Because I don't like euphemisms."

"Huh?"

"Putting a pretty word on something ugly. Body-checking! Sounds harmless, like checkers, but it means creaming the other guy."

"Yeah, but there are, like, rules. No elbows and you can't—"

"Zip it. I don't want to talk about hockey."

"So are we done? Can I go up to my room?"

Mom gazed at Bro. He'd been rocking, but now he stopped, the rocker going still, as though Mom had put the brakes on it with her eyes.

"Was it a sucker punch?" she said at last.

"No way!" said Bro. "I told you and told you."

"Tell me again."

"It wasn't a sucker punch. We dropped our helmets, Mom! That's the signal in hockey."

"Signal for what?"

"Throwing down."

Mom went on gazing at Bro, then finally nodded. "We don't sucker punch in this family."

"I know that, Mom."

She pointed her finger at him. "And we don't punch at all, except in the most extreme circumstances."

"Like what?" Bro said.

"Like today," said Mom.

A smile spread slowly across Bro's face. "Thanks, Mom." Bro jumped up.

"Not so fast," Mom said. "Where do you think you're going?"

"Upstairs."

Mom shook her head. "You're going outside to get your sister."

"But I told you—she took Arthur for a walk."

"It's been an hour," Mom said. "That's enough walking."

Bro went to the front door, opened it, and yelled, "Har-mon-y! Har-mon-y! Har—"

He stopped when he noticed what I had seen the moment he'd opened the door. A woman wearing a short leather jacket and jeans was coming up the walk. Behind her in our circular drive, a man at the wheel of a parked car was watching. He had a trimmed, reddish beard. Beards are whiskers, unless I'm mistaken, and don't put your money on that. I've got whiskers, too, of course, but mine are adorable.

Bro backed away. The woman came in. She wore shiny high-heeled boots. Lots of women in these parts wear boots, but not the high-heeled kind. She glanced around, her eyes—almost lost in all that makeup—sweeping over Bro and not even coming near me—how strange!—and finally falling on Mom.

"Is this the Blueberry Hill Inn?" the woman said.

"Blackberry," said Mom.

"Whatever," the woman said. "I'm picking up Sasha's stuff."

"I'm sorry?" Mom said.

"Didn't you get the text? Sasha LeMaire? His stuff? Suitcase? Et cetera?"

"Ah," said Mom. "His first name is Alex in the register."

"So? Sasha's a nickname for Alex. Is that news out here?"

"Out here?"

"In the boonies."

Mom smiled. She has several smiles, all nice to look at, although this one, where her eyes don't join in, sends a cold message. Mom's cold smile—never directed at me, of course—is a rare sight that I always enjoy.

"You learn something every day," Mom said. She wheeled Mr. LeMaire's suitcase out from behind the desk. "I'll just need to see some ID."

"Excuse me?" said the woman.

And here was Mom's cold smile again. What an entertaining day we were having so far! "Can't release guest property to a third party without an ID."

"Third party?"

"The inn being party one, and Mr. Alex 'Sasha' LeMaire party two."

"What the—didn't you get the—his text?"

"No problem there," Mom said. "So let's get the ID step taken care of and you'll be on your way back to civilization."

Was it possible that this woman didn't like Mom? What an odd stance to take in life, but I got that impression from the look on her face. She muttered something that sounded like, "It's in the car," then turned and walked out, closing the door firmly behind her.

"What's goin' on?" Bro said.

"Bad manners," said Mom.

They waited. I waited in a different way, due to the fact that from my command post I could see through the fanlight window over the door right out to the circular drive. The driver-side window was down and the red-bearded man and the woman in the high-heeled boots were having a conversation; snapping at each other, in fact, although I couldn't make out the words. Finally the man took out a stack of card-like things, rifled through them, and handed one to the woman. She headed back our way and moments later flipped the card-like thing onto the desk.

"Thank you, Ms."—Mom read the name on the card—"Jones." She copied the card in the copy machine, handed it to Ms. Jones, and rolled the suitcase to her. "Enjoy the day."

"Sure," said Ms. Jones, and left again, with another firm closing of the door.

Mom took a sheet of paper from the copier and read out loud: "Ms. Mary A. Jones, 419B Zither Street, Brooklyn, New York."

"Ever been to New York, Mom?" Bro said.

"Once," said Mom. "I'll tell you all about it after you come back."

"From what?"

"Getting Harmony. Now scoot."

"Can I eat something first? I'm starving."

"Take a snack with you. Move."

Bro headed for the kitchen. Through the fantail light, I saw that Ms. Jones hadn't left yet. She was standing by the car, where the red-bearded man had the suitcase open on the trunk and was going through the contents. Then they snapped at each other some more, and Ms. Jones came our way again. Humans snap at each other from time to time, some more than others. I prefer those who keep a lid on it. Meanwhile the man stuck the suitcase in the trunk and got back in the car. He put on one of those hats with big earflaps, the kind that hides most of the face when they're fastened. He fastened them.

Ms. Jones entered.

"You're back?" Mom said.

Ms. Jones gave us her smile for the first time. And now her voice changed, suddenly turning kind of sweet. It was like a new person. I decided I liked the old one better, but neither of them very much.

"Sorry to keep bothering you," she said, "but are you sure there was nothing else?" Ms. Jones did something with her eyelashes, called batting her eyes, if I recall. We don't see it often out here in the boonies, just another one of our pleasant features. "In Sasha's luggage, I mean?"

"Like what?" Mom said.

Bro returned, eating one of Bertha's famous mocha brownies, famous at least here at the Blackberry Hill Inn.

"Oh, nothing important," said Ms. Jones. "Just a small thing. It might look like some folded-up paper or document."

Mom started to shake her head, but at that moment Bro got involved. He could be unpredictable at times. "Thrmm proombard," he said.

"Please don't speak with your mouth full," Mom said.

Bro got totally involved in chewing. It must have been a very big chunk of brownie because a long time seemed to go by before he said, "Don't forget about the postcard, Mom."

There was a long pause before Mom said, "Ah, yes. Thanks for the reminder."

"Postcard?" said Ms. Jones.

Mom took the postcard from a drawer behind the desk. "Fell out of the suitcase when we were closing it up." She handed the postcard to Ms. Jones.

Ms. Jones gave it a close but puzzled look, front and back, then slipped it in the back pocket of her jeans. "I was actually thinking of something a little different."

"Different how?" said Mom.

"More . . . more like a . . . or maybe I should say bigger." She held up her hands to show bigger, although my guess was we'd all gotten the idea, me, Mom, and Bro. "Yes," Ms. Jones went on, "bigger—and with lines on it."

"Lines?"

"Like markings, really. For roads and stuff. Towns. Rivers. Mountains."

"Do you mean a map?"

"That sort of thing."

Mom shook her head. "There's only the postcard."

"Well, then, um, thanks."

"You're welcome."

Ms. Jones went outside again. Through the fantail window, I saw her get in the car. She said something to the man. He made angry gestures at her. She made angry gestures back. What a snappish couple! They drove off, and none too soon.

Meanwhile Mom was staring at the door in a thoughtful way and Bro was polishing off the brownie.

"Um," he said. "The postcard."

Mom turned to him. "What about it?"

"You forgot it was in the drawer?"

Mom gave him a long look. "No."

Bro nodded. "That's what I'm thinking. Not then. Now."

Mom laughed. She went over and gave Bro a hug.

"What?" he said. "Did I do something wrong? Or right? Or . . ."

"I was being sneaky about the postcard," Mom said. "Why is it worth three hundred dollars to Mr. Mahovlich? Why did Ms. Jones come back for it?"

"But she didn't. She wanted the map."

Mom paused. "You're right."

"And Mr. LeMaire has a map, Mom. Harmony and I saw it."

"Speaking of whom," Mom said, letting go of Bro, "git."

Bro zipped up his jacket and opened the door. Coming up the walk was Harmony. So much action today, although none of it the money-making kind. She was with an ax-carrying guy who looked like . . . why, yes, Matty—a big favorite of mine. He has the most comfortable shoulders I've ever sat on. Also there was one other party, waddling along behind with his tongue hanging out. Not a pretty picture. I turned my attention on Harmony, and at that very instant she saw Mom and began to run, her arms outstretched.

TEN

QUEENIE

NORMALLY I'D BE SETTLING IN FOR A nap around now, most likely on my bed—the one I share with Harmony—where it's nice and quiet during the day. There's nothing like a good nap, especially a nap chock-full of exciting dreams. Dreams with birds in them are my personal favorite. But right now there was simply too much going on and I felt surprisingly wakeful, sitting on my bookcase shelf in the Big Room.

Before me and slightly below—as if this were all a play put on for my amusement . . . and why not? Was it possibly true? Could all of what we call life be just a performance for the amusement of me? What an interesting thought, so deep! But this was not the time for exploring deep thoughts. I turned my attention to the goings-on in the Big Room.

On the couch we had Mom sitting next to Harmony with her arm over Harmony's shoulder. Bro sat cross-legged on the chair by the fire tools, eating another mocha brownie. Matty stood with his back to the fireplace. And zonked out on the rug in front of the fire, all four paws extended straight out and therefore taking up as much space as possible, was the other party.

"So Hunzinger's out there now?" Mom was saying. "It's his jurisdiction after all?"

Matty's eyebrows rose. He has lovely eyebrows, beautifully shaped, not too thick, not too thin. In fact, all of him is the same way: just right. "Sure, it's his jurisdiction. Was that ever in doubt?"

"How did someone like him ever get to be sheriff?" Mom said.

Bertha stuck her head into the room. "Political influence," she said. "But don't let me interrupt."

"As for the sheriff being out there, he had to turn back at the cliff," Matty said. "Bum knee from high school football."

"Pah," said Bertha. "No Hunzinger ever played high school football or any other sport. Bone-laziest family in these here hills."

"So Deputy Carstairs is handling things," Matty went on. "He didn't look too happy about it—just got back from Disney World, not even unpacked."

"Boo-hoo," said Bertha.

Bro looked up. "Mr. LeMaire is dead?"

"For god's sake, Bro!" said Harmony. "Have you been listening?"

"Yeah. It's just, well . . . we were with him. On the trail and all. Like yesterday. He said he wouldn't be . . . what was it, Harm?"

"Needing us anymore."

Bro looked down at the floor. "So maybe he did, huh? Need us, I mean."

He turned to Mom. So did Harmony. For a moment I got the idea that Mom didn't know what to say. That would have been a first. But before I could find out one way or another, Matty spoke up. "It's a very good thing you guys weren't there. The medical examiner makes the final call, but Carstairs is pretty sure the cause of death wasn't a fall or a bear or anything like that."

Bertha put her hand to her chest. "It was murder?"

Matty nodded. "Struck with a blunt object, in Carstairs's opinion."

"But who would do a thing like that?" said Bertha. "And why?"

"I wonder . . . ," Mom said.

"Wonder what?" said Harmony.

"Well," Mom said, "while you were up on the mountain, we had this odd visit." Her eyes got a far-off look. "Much odder now."

"What do you mean, Mom?" Harmony said.

"Remember the text Mr. LeMaire sent—about sending

someone for his stuff? Well, they came. She came, that is. A woman named Mary Jones from Brooklyn. I actually don't know if she was alone. Bro? Can you help on this?"

"Huh?"

"Think back. You opened the door to go get Harmony. Then the woman came in. Did she have a car in the driveway?"

"She musta, right?"

"But did you see it?"

"I . . . think so."

"Was anyone in it?"

"Like who?"

"That's what I'm asking."

"Dunno."

"Why is it important?" Matty said.

Harmony sat up straight. "Because Mr. LeMaire's text said he'd gone home but he hadn't. He was dead on the mountain."

"Hey," said Bro. "That's like a contradiction."

"You got that right," said Matty. He turned to Mom. "What did she want, this woman from Brooklyn?"

"His things," Mom replied, "like the text said."

"Especially the map," said Bro.

"Map?" said Harmony.

"Belonging to Mr. LeMaire," Mom said.

Harmony gave Bro a look. "Bro? You blabbed about the map?"

"Huh?"

"Sorry," Harmony said. "Of course you don't know. You weren't there. Sometimes when you're not around I still get the feeling you're around."

Bro nodded, like he understood what she was talking about.

"Mind clueing the rest of us in, Harmony?" Mom said. "What map?"

"Uh, nothing, Mom. It's not important."

"I'm waiting," Mom said.

Harmony sighed. "I don't want to rat him out, and besides, no one will believe it."

"Rat who out?" said Mom. "Nobody will believe what?"

Harmony glanced over at a certain party, snoozing his life away by the fire, not a care in the world. "Arthur ate the map," she said.

Matty laughed. "The old dog-ate-the-homework ploy."

"Exactly," said Harmony. "No one will ever buy it."

And then came a long saga of an adventure in a clearing up on Mount Misty. Pretty soon all eyes were on the sleeper. He remained oblivious. This saga was filled with twists and turns, but one thing for sure. The part about the map and who ate it? I believed it, totally. He was capable of doing the exact wrong thing at the—no, let me change that. He specialized in doing the exact wrong thing at the exact wrong moment. I was so busy glaring at the offender with my golden glare that I almost missed the sound of the front door opening. I turned slightly, bringing the hall into view from my spot on the top shelf, and saw two men in uniform. The tall one with the sunburned nose was Deputy Carstairs, often seen here at the inn because of his daughter Emma being friends with Harmony. The short, round one with the bushy mustache I'd seen only once—something about a guest, an ice storm, and a fender bender—but I remembered, probably because the bushy mustache pretty much covered his mouth, the sort of detail you want to forget but can't. This gentleman was Sheriff Hunzinger.

They entered the Big Room. "Sorry to barge in, Yvette," said Deputy Carstairs, Yvette being one of Mom's other names. Mrs. Reddy is another, and there's also Ms. Reddy. That strikes me as a bit confusing. I'm Queenie, and that's that.

"I'm sure you've heard about this . . . incident up on Mount Misty," the deputy went on. He glanced at Harmony, and in a gentle voice said, "How you doing?"

"All right," said Harmony.

"You did good up there," the deputy said.

Mom patted Harmony's hand. A nice sight, and everyone was taking it in, with the exception of Sheriff Hunzinger. His eyes were on Matty.

"We've got some questions about this guest of yours, Alex LeMaire," the deputy said.

"Is it true he was murdered?" Mom said.

"Have to wait on the ME for that," said the deputy. "But—"

Hunzinger interrupted, his mustache sort of billowing in the breeze of his own speech, like a hairy curtain. "I don't have to wait one darn minute. Murder for sure. So for starters, how about filling us in on what this city fella was doing up there?"

"He just wanted to hike the old Sokoki Trail," Mom said. "Other than that he didn't say much."

"Any idea what had him interested in that particular trail?" said Carstairs.

Mom shook her head.

"No mention of digging up Colonial artifacts?" said Hunzinger.

"Colonial artifacts?" said Mom.

Hunzinger turned to Matty. "Maybe our archaeologist buddy here can explain."

"I'm not an archaeologist," Matty said.

"No? Word is you got an advanced degree."

"Nice to know my background's of general interest," Matty said. A remark that made Bro snicker. I'd never heard him snicker, and if you'd asked me whether he'd even been following this conversation, my answer would have been no. But Bro can be unpredictable, as I've mentioned before. Was he growing more unpredictable? I'd have to mull that over some other time. Right now Matty was saying, ". . . a few undergraduate courses, that's it."

"That'd be a few more'n me," Hunzinger said. "So maybe you can . . ." He turned to Carstairs. "What's the word I'm lookin' for?"

"Not sure where you're going with this, sheriff," said Carstairs, wrinkling up his nose. Emma did the same thing, and on her it was cute. In the deputy's case, his nose being so sunburned and rather large for a human, not so cute. I had a sudden urge to look in a mirror, but none were in my line of sight.

The sheriff snapped his fingers. I'm no fan of finger snapping in general, and this kind, like a gunshot, was particularly unlikable. "Enlighten! That's the word. Maybe you can enlighten us on how trained archaeologists feel about random folks comin' in to dig stuff up."

"I don't understand," Mom said. "What stuff are you talking about?"

"Trading post stuff," said the sheriff. "Muskets,

blankets, pots and pans, beads—from this trading post up on the old Sokoki Trail going back to Colonial days, and the French before that."

"There's no proof a trading post even existed," Matty said. "The records are sparse and really vague."

"But some folks believe it," Hunzinger said. "This LeMaire character wouldn't be the first to come diggin' around. So enlighten us on how archaeologists feel about folks like him."

Matty has interesting blue eyes, sometimes deep blue and sometimes more icy blue. Right now they were icy blue. He gazed at Hunzinger and said, "I can't speak for all archaeologists."

"How's about yourself?" said Hunzinger. Carstairs did his nose-wrinkling thing again, as though smelling something bad.

"I can speak for myself," Matty said. "I don't like people coming to dig stuff up."

"Aha!" said the sheriff.

But at the same instant, Carstairs was saying, "Why is that?"

"Huh?" Hunzinger said. "What's the point of going there?"

Carstairs took a deep breath. Before he could say anything, Matty said, "Because they hurt the environment, ruin the sites, and make the science impossible. Archaeologists aren't interested in making money off artifacts. All they want to do is understand the past."

"Say again?" said Hunzinger.

Matty said it again. Since I'd caught it the first time, I didn't listen, instead imagining some alternate world where I was the sheriff and this was all moving along much quicker.

"'Kay," the sheriff said. "I get the gist. We're all on board?"

"For what?" said Mom.

Hunzinger turned to her. "How about if I told you that before checking in here to your place, Mr. LeMaire spent some time over at the library, talking to old Mrs. Hale?"

"Go on," Mom said.

"And in that conversation he asked what she knew about any digging that had gone on over the years on the old Sokoki Trail."

Mom looked at the sheriff and didn't say anything.

"Mrs. Hale being the resident town historian, if you follow," the sheriff said.

Mom remained silent. That's usually my policy as well.

"Point being," the sheriff continued, now focusing on Matty, "that Mr. LeMaire was all psyched on the subject of artifacts. Any reaction to that, Matty?"

Matty's eyes got icier. The sheriff's mustache fluttered a bit, like maybe some sort of smile was going on underneath that mustache. I've never bitten a human—well, never say never—but I was getting a strong impulse. My teeth are not ridiculously oversized, like the teeth of a certain party I won't name—but they are extremely sharp.

"No," Matty said. "No reaction."

Then came a long silence when everyone seemed to be waiting for the sheriff to speak, and he seemed to be waiting for who knows what. At last Carstairs said, "Perhaps we could move on to that other matter."

The sheriff blinked. "Other matter?"

Carstairs leaned over and whispered in the sheriff's ear. A large and hairy ear. You might say that I myself am covered in hair of a sort, but the effect in my case could not be more different. Oh, and by the way, what Carstairs whispered was, "The map." Human whispers are a snap to pick up, at least with hearing like mine. A certain party also has good hearing—I'll give him that—but what good does it do when you're off in dreamland?

ELEVEN

ARTHUR

WE WERE OUT IN THE BACK GARDEN on a nice summer day. Bertha was grilling thick steaks on the barbecue and I was keeping her company. Thick and juicy steaks, the kind, I think, that's called a ribeye. Or possibly a New York strip. That doesn't really matter because I've never tasted steak I didn't like. And *like* isn't even the word. *Love* is the word. I've never tasted steak I didn't love.

Bertha flipped one over. Sizzle sizzle. "This one's for you, Arthur," she said. "You like 'em rare, don't you?"

Yes!

"Or is it medium rare?"

Yes!

"Or medium?"

Yes! Yes, yes, and yes! I was yessing away with all I had in me when I woke up. Why did that have to happen? I didn't have to pee or anything like that, and even if I did, which was sort of the case, now that I thought about it,

I'm great at holding on. Also, I was still plenty tuckered out from whatever it was I'd been doing earlier. So why was I awake?

I opened my eyes. What was this? We had a sort of crowd situation in the Big Room? Guests at last! That had to be a good thing. Then I noticed that I knew some of these guests, like Matty and Deputy Carstairs, so they probably weren't guests. The dude I didn't know was kind of scary, with a huge mustache that hid his mouth. It didn't take me long to spot the fact that he was wearing a uniform, and not only that but a uniform not unlike the deputy's, the color of some puke I'd once puked up after snacking on a bowl of pickled olives, a one-time event as I promised myself then, although it had kind of happened again. But the point was that very quickly I was totally on top of the situation in the Big Room, and all this while still lying comfortably in front of the fire. Sometimes I amaze myself.

"The other matter," this mustached dude was saying, "concerns a map."

Mom, sitting beside Harmony on the couch—a couch called an antique, by the way, that I'm not allowed to sit on, a detail that turns out to be surprisingly hard to remember—paused before saying, "Map, Sheriff?"

Aha! The mustache dude was the sheriff! Bertha talks about him from time to time, always using strong language. I was following along just perfectly! They seemed to be talking about a map. That didn't sound too interesting, but maybe they'd quickly move on to something else.

"What sort of map?" Mom said.

"You tell me," said the sheriff.

"Excuse me?" said Mom.

"I believe what Sheriff Hunzinger meant to say," Deputy Carstairs said, "is that old Mrs. Hale down at the library had shown Mr. LeMaire a map. Evidently he made a copy. We were just wondering if you knew anything about it?"

"But why would I?" Mom said.

Good for Mom! Why would she know anything about some map? Why would any of us? I certainly didn't.

"The thing is, Yvette," Carstairs said, "no map was found on the body. That seemed a bit strange to us—why have a map if you don't take it with you?"

How complicated that sounded, way above my pay grade, as Bertha likes to say. Bertha and I are great buddies. We spend lots of time together. In the kitchen.

"Map's got to be somewheres," the sheriff said. "Unless the dog ate it. Heh heh." He slapped his thigh and said it again: "Unless the dog ate it." The sheriff laughed some more, as though something funny was going on.

Carstairs, standing slightly behind the sheriff, rolled his eyes—an always-interesting human trick—and said, "That's a good one, Sheriff."

107

"Knew you'd like it," the sheriff said. "So any info you can help us with, Mrs. Reddy?"

Mom didn't answer right away. She seemed to be looking my way, in fact directly at me. And so were Harmony, Bro, and Matty, all of them looking at me. That was very friendly of them. I raised my tail and thumped it down on the rug, which is how I wag while in a reclining position. Mom turned to the sheriff.

"All I can tell you is you're not the first one to ask about this map," she said.

"Let me guess," the sheriff said. "Was the first one this gentleman, by any chance?" He pointed his finger straight at Matty.

"Actually it wasn't," Mom said. She folded her arms across her chest. Sometimes Harmony does the same thing. My way of doing it is by digging in my heels. I can make myself just about impossible to move, always a fun time.

"Mind telling us who the person was, Yvette?" Carstairs said. "If you please?"

"I don't mind telling you, Al," Mom said. And she started in on a story about a text, a woman from Brooklyn, a suitcase, and a whole lot of other stuff that flew by at a great distance, like a flock of birds high in the sky. I myself have no interest in birds, although I have an acquaintance who does. I glanced up at her on her stupid bookshelf, looking down on us like . . . like she was above it all! Just once I'd like to . . . but then I remind myself, Arthur, think of the speed of those claws and the way you don't know what hit you till it's all over, and then I settle down.

Meanwhile Carstairs was saying, "Mind getting that address for us?"

"Not at all," Mom said. She went out to the hall, came back with a sheet of paper, and handed it to the deputy.

He read it out loud. " 'Ms. Mary A. Jones, 419B Zither Street, Brooklyn, New York.' That should be helpful." He moved to the far side of the room and got on his phone.

At just about the same time, the sheriff's phone buzzed. He answered, "This is the sheriff," then listened, said, "Thanks much," and stuck the phone in his pocket. "That was the ME," he said, in that strange, mouthless way he had of talking. "Cause of death—blow from behind with a blunt instrument. In other words, murder."

He gazed at Matty. Matty gazed back at him. How long that would have gone on was anybody's guess, but we got lucky and Carstairs soon came back, putting his own phone away.

"There is no Zither Street in Brooklyn. I'm afraid the ID was fake, Yvette."

"Can't say I'm surprised," the sheriff said.

"Oh," said Mom. "I certainly am."

"On account of you being a civilian." The sheriff tapped the side of his nose. "I've been smelling something fishy from day one."

Wow! What a surprise! The truth was this sheriff dude had not been making a good first impression on me. But now it turned out he could smell things I couldn't? I sniffed the air: not a single trace of fish, and fish is one of the easiest smells out there, along with bacon and . . . and more bacon. And yet he somehow smelled fish? I made up my mind then and there to keep a close eye on Sheriff Hunzinger.

At that moment Harmony piped up. "When was day one?" she said.

The sheriff gave her a look that some adults give kids when they pipe up. "Huh?" he said. "Not sure I get your question."

"Uh, I think the answer has to be 'today,' right, Sheriff?" said Carstairs. "Today being when the body was found and all."

"So?" said the sheriff.

Which was when Bro jumped in. What was going on? Bro never jumps into this kind of thing. Then it occurred to me that we'd never had this kind of thing before. What an amazing thought by me, far beyond my usual type of thoughts. And just when I had that thought, the first one, so amazing, vanished in a way that felt like forever. Thinking beyond my usual thoughts turned out to be very tiring. I hoped it wouldn't happen again, at least not for a while.

But back to what Bro said, namely, "So you just started smelling something fishy today?"

The sheriff looked at Bro, then at Harmony, then back to Bro. "You kids wouldn't be makin' fun of me, now would you?"

Bro opened his mouth like he was about to say something, but then Harmony shook her head and Bro shook his head, too. All I knew was that I still smelled nothing fishy.

Carstairs rubbed his hands together. "Moving right along, then, how about we get started on the next phase?"

"Of what?" said the sheriff.

"The investigation," Carstairs said.

"Exactly my point." The sheriff took a notebook from his chest pocket and flipped through the pages, then nodded to himself. "Next phase being the search."

"What search?" Mom said.

"We'd like your permission to search the room where LeMaire stayed," Carstairs told her.

"Of course," Mom said, rising. "It's upstairs."

"Is there an elevator?" the sheriff said.

"Afraid not," said Mom.

"Why don't you handle the search, Al?" the sheriff said. He took out his phone. "I'll check ongoing developments at the station."

Mom led Carstairs out of the Big Room toward the stairs. The next moment I found myself up and on my feet, trailing after them. Why? I had no clue, but that didn't make it a bad idea, not in my experience.

"Nice room," said Carstairs.

We were in the room at the end of the hall, the room with the balcony and the view of Mount Misty, now clouded over so there was no view.

"Thanks," Mom said.

Carstairs looked around. What was he searching for again? Had someone mentioned it? I searched my mind, found not much going on at the moment. But I certainly didn't smell fish, if that was what this was all about.

"I have a method for this," Carstairs said, getting down on his knees, which made a cracking sound I've heard before from the human knee, but never from me and my kind. Do we even have knees? I wasn't sure. "Stole it from a detective novel—whenever you're searching a room, start from the bottom up."

"You're a reader, Al?"

"When I can fit it in."

Carstairs raised the edge of the bedspread, stuck his head under the bed, and peered around.

"Hey, Arthur," he said. "What's up, buddy?"

Not much. I found myself right at the deputy's side. Whenever a human gets down on all fours—the only way to go, in my opinion—I like to encourage them.

Deputy Carstairs and I checked out what was under the bed, which turned out to be nothing, not even dust balls. We had standards here at the Blackberry Hill Inn— something Bertha says a lot.

"Are you looking for anything in particular?" Mom said from up above.

"Not really," Carstairs said. His eyes shifted over in my direction. Were those eyes trying to tell me something? I wondered about that, and immediately got nowhere. Carstairs backed out from under the bed and rose. Next he went to the chest of drawers and started opening them, bottom drawer first. Over his shoulder he said, "My divorce came through last month."

"Emma mentioned that," Mom said.

"She's a good kid."

"That's an understatement."

Carstairs grunted. "Tough on kids, no matter what anyone says."

113

Mom gazed at Carstairs's back and didn't say anything.

Was the search still going on? I wasn't sure, but then Carstairs went into the bathroom and looked behind the shower curtain, so I guessed that it was. After that, he checked the little closet under the sink, the medicine cabinet, and even that tank thingy behind the toilet, where Bertha sometimes rattles the insides around when the guests have plumbing problems, never a good moment here at the Blackberry Hill Inn. Carstairs glanced in the toilet bowl, empty, and flushed it anyway, and then left the room. I lingered behind: toilet bowl water just after flushing is extremely tasty, something you may not know.

"Is that it?" Mom was saying to Carstairs when I emerged from the bathroom, feeling refreshed.

Carstairs glanced around. "I'll just check the balcony," he said. He crossed the room, opened the door, and stepped outside. A cold breeze swept into the room. Mom looked my way.

"Why are you drooling?"

Me? How embarrassing! I gave my muzzle a good lick, made everything right.

Meanwhile, out on the balcony, Carstairs was moving a few folded-up lawn chairs. He went still and said, "Hmm." When he came back in, he was carrying a bottle of golden-colored liquid.

"What's that?" Mom said.

He showed her the bottle, a real dirty bottle, reminding me of toys I've buried all over the yard. "'Maple Leaf Gold Canadian rye whisky,'" he said. "Any sign of LeMaire being a drinking man?"

"Not that I saw," Mom said. She peered at the bottle. "It looks old."

Carstairs rubbed away some of the dirt. "Seal's still in place, so he hadn't started in on it. Any empties found in the room?"

Mom shook her head, then took another look at the bottle. "The label's kind of faded."

"Maybe he left it out in the sun," said Carstairs.

We went downstairs, and Carstairs showed Hunzinger the bottle.

"Well, well," said the sheriff. "Half in the bag and wandering around the mountain, huh? Makes an easy target."

"No question about that," Carstairs said, "but do we know for a fact that he had a drinking prob—"

The sheriff interrupted. "Meaning an easy target for someone sneaking up from behind, carrying let's say an ax. Back side of an ax head's what you might call blunt." He smiled a little smile. Most human smiles are nice to see. Others are just about showing teeth. This smile was one of those. "Speaking of axes, Matty, my friend, Deputy

Carstairs happened to mention that you were carrying one, up on the mountain."

Matty shrugged. "Part of my job, clearing trails after storms."

"Is that so?" said the sheriff. "And while you were busy with that, did you maybe bump into this LeMaire fella digging around for Colonial art-ee-facts? Messing up the science and spoiling the environment? We recovered his backpack in that little shelter up there. Happened to have a fold-up shovel inside."

Matty, sitting on a footstool by the fireplace, changed his position slightly, his feet now more under him. "The first time I laid eyes on Mr. LeMaire was when Harmony showed me the body," he said, his voice nice and calm.

"Sure, sure," the sheriff said. "No one's saying that any-thing was premeditated. But you did mention that you're no fan of the kind of outsiders who make a buck by digging up stuff. It's wrong. Dead wrong. I get that. Throw into the mix that this city slicker was also a juicer and likely said or did some reckless things, taking a swing at you with his shovel, for example. Might even end up with a self-defense situation when the trial rolls around."

"Trial?" said Mom. "For goodness' sake, Sheriff, what are you saying?"

The sheriff smiled that nasty smile again. The next thing I knew I was on my feet. Why? I had no idea. I was still pretty tired, in fact.

"Matty," he said. "How about you explain to Mrs. Reddy here?"

Matty rose. "You're out of your mind," he said. "And even worse, you're lazy and stupid. That's the only explanation I can think of."

The sheriff's face went bright red. He put his hand on the butt of his gun. Carstairs touched the sheriff's shoulder. "Sheriff? A quick word?"

The sheriff shrugged him off. "Later, Al. Right now we're taking him in." He took out handcuffs, moved toward Matty. "This can be hard or it can be easy, Matty. Your call."

"I'm not going anywhere. This is a fantasy. You have no evidence."

"That's not for you to say," the sheriff said. "And in case it's slipped your mind, you've been in trouble with the law before."

Harmony and Bro looked at each other in surprise.

"For hunting out of season, for god's sake," Matty said. "And that was ten years ago. I've changed my thinking since then."

"Maybe," the sheriff said, "but it's on your record."

Now they were face-to-face.

"Turn and place your hands behind you," the sheriff said.

"I won't do it," said Matty.

"Yes you will," the sheriff said, and he grabbed Matty with his free hand and tried to spin him around.

Matty wouldn't be spun around. He pushed the sheriff, not a hard push, but somehow hard enough to knock him down.

"Al!" the sheriff shouted.

Matty took off, sprinting toward the front hall. Carstairs, surprisingly quick, blocked his way. Matty swerved and raced to the doors that led to the patio.

"Halt!" the sheriff called.

Matty didn't even pause. He banged those doors open and bolted outside. But what was this? The sheriff, stumbling to his feet and drawing his gun, with Matty framed between the open doors? My teeth felt this enormous urge, by far the most powerful urge that had ever possessed them, stronger than any power on earth. In short, what was about to happen couldn't be stopped.

TWELVE

QUEENIE

WHAT A SITUATION, UNUSUAL IN many ways. One of those ways had to do with the doors to the Big Room—French doors, I believe they are called—now wide open. I filed that little tidbit away for later.

Meanwhile, Matty was no longer in sight, although Deputy Carstairs could still be seen, perhaps chasing after him, if that's what his slow-motion running through the snowy back meadow was all about. In the Big Room we had a lot of drama going on with Sheriff Hunzinger, who had rolled up his pant leg and was moaning in pain. All I could see was what looked like a scratch on his skinny calf. A disappointingly tiny little scratch: Bertha knelt and dabbed at it with a paper towel.

"There," she said. "All better."

"All better? What are you talking about?" The sheriff's voice, never pleasant to my ears, had risen to a kind of shriek. "Has it had its shots?"

"We think of Arthur as a he," Mom said. "But yes, of course he's had his shots. And he barely broke the surface."

The sheriff lurched away, shook his finger at Mom and Bertha. "The ugly cur bit me, plain and simple. That's assault!"

"I'm sure he didn't mean—"

The sheriff's voice overwhelmed Mom's. "He's going to regret it! You're all going to regret it!"

Mom turned to Harmony and Bro. "Kids? Can you get Arthur out of here?"

As for Arthur, where to even begin? Certainly not with what he was doing at the moment, namely prancing around the Big Room with that ridiculous stubby tail of his wagging nonstop. Why had he done what he'd done? What had gone on in his mind? Anything? I really had no idea. But I was very pleased with Arthur. Even if I couldn't believe I was thinking such a thought.

The kids rounded up Arthur—no one easier to round up—and hustled him out of the Big Room. A few moments later the sheriff, shouting orders into his phone, was gone, too. He hit the siren right away, a sound that does terrible things to my ears. More to get away from the siren than anything else—anything to do with birds, for example—I made my silent way down from the bookshelf, across the Big Room, and toward the French doors, framing the view

120

in a very pretty way. The bird feeder was part of that view; no one could help noticing that detail, even a peaceful type whose only interest was getting away from the noise and possibly stretching her legs a little.

The French doors closed, practically in my face. Mom looked down. "Nice try, cutie."

Big Fred came over not long after that. Always interesting to see Big Fred. I especially like how he ducks when going in and out of rooms, but still manages to hit his head on something or other up above, like ceilings. Big Fred is Bertha's boyfriend and also the boss of the volunteer fire department, meaning he has a police scanner.

"Any news, Freddie?" Bertha said. She calls him Freddie, like he's a little kid, but no little kid ever had a voice like Big Fred's, a low rumble I could feel in my paws, all the way up on the bookshelf—and a very nice sound, by the way, almost the opposite of sirens.

He shook his head. "Looks like Matty got himself clean away, for now. Al Carstairs is back at the station; lost one of his boots in the snow. Sheriff's gone to the hospital."

"Hospital?" Mom said.

"For tests, he said." Big Fred glanced over at a certain party, now back to dozing by the fire. "How bad was the bite?"

"Oh, good grief," Bertha said. "Couldn't call it a bite. Hardly even a scratch."

Big Fred nodded. "Kind of what I thought."

"Meanwhile," Mom said, "what about Matty?"

"He shouldn't ought to have run," Big Fred said. "Is it true he assaulted the sheriff?"

"Assault?" said Bertha. "He hardly touched him. The sheriff was going to cuff him, Freddie! On these completely bogus charges."

"Shouldn't ought to have touched the sheriff," Big Fred said. "And the longer he's in the wind, the worse it's going to be."

"Then let's go find him!" Harmony said.

Big Fred turned to Harmony and smiled. "Find Matty Comeau somewheres in these mountains when he doesn't want to be found? Good luck with that."

"Um," Bro said.

Everyone turned to him.

"Something on your mind?" said Big Fred. "Heard you popped Foster Mahovlich a good one, by the way."

"Please, Fred," Mom said.

"Sorry."

"Uh, if we can't find Matty," Bro said, and then came to a halt.

"Go on," Mom said.

Bro shrugged. "I don't know. It's just an idea."

"Lost me a bit there, son," said Big Fred.

Bro looked down, maybe like he'd had an unhappy thought. Just to clear up any possible confusion, Big Fred is not Bro's dad. Dad is Bro's dad. He hasn't been seen around these parts in some time. Neither has Lilah Fairbanks, the interior decorator Mom hired to fix things up nice and fancy. Now the decor is back to how it was.

"Tell us about this idea," Mom said, her voice gentle.

"It's stupid," Bro said.

"No it's not," said Harmony. "Bro's thinking that since Matty could never have murdered Mr. LeMaire then someone else did. So all we have to do is find that someone else and then Matty will be off the hook."

"Yeah," Bro said. "Like that."

"Whoa!" said Big Fred. "They read each other's minds?"

"Not all the time, thank god." Mom turned to Bro. "A very smart thought," she said. "If a bit impracticable."

"What's impracticable?" said Bro.

"Not easy to actually do in real life," Harmony said.

"So?" said Bro. "We've got to do something. In real life they're—"

Harmony chimed in, their voices blending together. "—trying to put Matty in jail!"

Mom gave them a careful look. "Kids?" she said.

■ ■ ■

That night things were very quiet at the Blackberry Hill Inn. After supper, we all gathered in the guest lounge, which was where the TV was. The TV wasn't on. Harmony and I were sprawled on an old corduroy chair, very comfy, that Big Fred had rescued from a furniture store fire down at the discount mall, Harmony reading a book and me watching her read. Her eyes went back and forth, back and forth in a way I couldn't not watch. Bro was staring into nowhere, which is what he does instead of reading, and Mom was examining the dusty bottle of Maple Leaf Gold Canadian rye whisky.

"Think it's any good?" she said.

"Hey!" said Bro, suddenly coming out of his trance or whatever it was. "You like whisky, Mom?"

"Not so far in this life," Mom said. "Maybe it's time to start, in a big way."

Harmony looked up. "Mom?"

Mom laughed. "Actually, I was thinking that if it was any good we could give it to somebody for Christmas."

"A . . . murder victim's bottle?" Harmony said, her voice quiet.

"There is that," said Mom, her voice going quiet, too.

"Look it up," Bro said, his voice staying the same, kind of cheerful.

124

"What?" said Mom.

"The whisky. Online. To see if it's good. There'll be reviews, like for everything else."

Mom opened her laptop, started tapping away. "Funny," she said after some time.

"No reviews?" Bro said.

"Not only that," said Mom, "but they stopped making it in 1933."

"Meaning that's a real old bottle," Harmony said.

"Worth a lot of money?" said Bro. "Like to collectors?"

"Are there whisky collectors?" Harmony said.

"I don't know," said Mom.

"Maybe we should crack 'er open, give it a taste," Bro said.

"It's your bedtime," said Mom.

Snow fell again that night. Snow pitter-pattering on the roof is the best sleeping sound there is. Harmony's hair was spread across the pillow, so convenient. I curled up on her hair and after that don't remember a thing until morning, when we awoke to the sound of commotion going on below.

We went downstairs, rubbing our eyes. Well, Harmony was rubbing her eyes. Mine never need rubbing, just another reason, if you're keeping track, why it's nice to be me. And my way of going down stairs is probably much different than yours. I sort of flow down, like a small, beautiful wave. I wish I could see myself doing it. Is there some sort of mirror that could follow me around? Humans invent all sorts of things—most of them useless, in my opinion—so why not that?

In the front hall we had Mom and a stranger, plus a certain party, standing by his water bowl and gazing at nothing. "Mind in neutral," as Dad used to say, although he said it about Bro. I didn't miss Dad.

We get some ex-hippies in these parts. The men usually rock the gray-ponytail bald-on-top look, sometimes with a beard, sometimes with long furry sideburns. The stranger in the hall was the sideburn type. He also wore a uniform, not the pukey green kind sported by the sheriff and his deputy but a pukey khaki, mud-stained here and there. He was carrying a leash. Meanwhile I'd left out the most important detail: Mom was upset. I could tell from the way her neck had gone all pink, and how rigidly she was standing.

"Is this a joke?" she said.

The stranger shook his head. "Just doin' my job, ma'am."

"There's no more pitiful excuse than that," said Mom.

The stranger shrugged, took some paperwork from his chest pocket. "Got the duly executed authority, if you'd care to take a look."

Mom reached out and grabbed the paperwork. Her eyes went back and forth, got more and more upset.

"Mom?" said Harmony. "What's going on?"

Mom spoke to Harmony but her eyes—her glaring eyes—were on the stranger. "This is Mr. Immler. He's the county animal control officer. There's been a complaint about Arthur."

"Huh? From who?"

"The sheriff. He sent Mr. Immler here to take Arthur into custody."

"Not custody," said Mr. Immler. "That's not the verbiage we use. Any complaint concerning a dangerous animal requires me to remove said animal for a period of observation."

"Arthur?" said Harmony. "A dangerous animal?"

We all looked over at a certain party, catching him mid-yawn.

"Won't take more'n a week or two. Then, if he checks out all right, you get him back safe and sound."

"Back from where?" Harmony said.

"County shelter," said Mr. Immler.

"No way!" Harmony said, her face reddening. "He'd have to be with other dogs?"

"Mostly pit bulls. Couple Rottweilers. And a Weimaraner came in yesterday, probable sheep killer."

One of the little quirks about a certain party is that he prefers not to be around members of his own kind, the more the worse. Harmony ran over and scooped him up, catching him by surprise. He was delighted, and started licking her face super energetically.

"There's a hard way for doing this and an easy way," Mr. Immler said.

"I'm calling my lawyer," said Mom.

"Your privilege. But I'm removing the animal now."

Mr. Immler advanced on Harmony and . . . what was he in this situation? The unwary victim? Something like that. Harmony held the unwary victim tight. Mr. Immler held out the clip for fastening the collar to the leash, but just when he was about to snap it into place, Harmony twisted away, ran to the door, threw it open, and put the unwary victim down in the snow.

"Run, Arthur, run!"

Instead he rolled over and played dead, a good trick, although his only one. In a flash Mr. Immler was on the scene, swooping down and clipping him to the leash. He led the victim—no longer unwary, but it was way too late for that—toward a van waiting in the circle.

Harmony raced after them, screaming and crying. Arthur—oh, Arthur!—dug in his feet, so oversized given the rest of him, but it did no good. For one scary moment, it looked like Harmony was about to leap onto Mr. Immler's back, but Mom caught up and pulled her away. A moment after that, the van was driving away, with Arthur shut up in the back, out of sight.

They walked back inside, Mom with her arm around Harmony's shoulders. Tears streamed down Harmony's face. Mom was crying, too, a rare sight, unseen by me since the last days of Dad. Meanwhile Bro was coming down the stairs, rubbing his eyes in the exact same way Harmony did, although with a smear of drool on his cheek as an added touch.

"Yo," he said, "what's shakin'?"

An excellent question. For some reason, what was shaking seemed to be me. Just slightly—certainly not noticeable—and I was sure this strangeness would quickly pass. But it was real. There are mysteries in life.

Not long after that, Deputy Carstairs arrived.

"Oh, good," Mom said. "You're here to clear up this ridiculous situation with Arthur."

Carstairs looked down at his feet. "I'm sorry, Yvette. I tried."

"Then why are you here?"

Wow! Mom was mad! Carstairs actually flinched.

"I've come for the bottle," he said. "The old bottle of whisky. It may be evidence in the case and—"

Mom whirled around, got the bottle from behind the desk, thrust it into Carstairs's hands so hard he almost lost his balance.

"Yvette," he said, looking very upset. "Please."

"You can show yourself out," Mom said.

THIRTEEN

ARTHUR

I WAS IN A VERY SMALL ROOM WITH A LOW ceiling, cement floor, and concrete blocks for walls, except for the front wall, which was made of metal bars too close together for squeezing through. Well, I could actually fit my head through the bars, just not the rest of me. I'd tried the moment I was left alone. And I tried again after that. And again and again and again. If only the rest of me was smaller! Was it true that I was on the roly-poly side? What did that mean? I'd always thought roly poly was a good thing, on account of how Bro and Harmony always smiled when they said it. I missed Bro and Harmony real bad. I missed Mom. I missed Bertha. I missed my home at the Blackberry Hill Inn. I even missed Queenie.

All I wanted to do right now, if I couldn't get out of here, was to lie down and sleep and maybe dream of home. But it wasn't safe to lie down. Did I mention something about being alone? That wasn't quite right. I had company in my very small room, company that went by the name of

Drogan, which was what Mr. Immler had called him when he'd put me in the room.

"Here's a buddy for you, Drogan. Take real good care of him."

Drogan was one of my kind but a lot different, maybe twice my size, and with teeth that always showed, even when his mouth was closed. But the scary part was the look in his eyes. Drogan was angry, angry all the time. Right now he was lying in one of the back corners, watching me, but the moment I lay down and closed my eyes, he'd rise and slink across the floor, and then I'd feel his hot breath on my face and open my eyes, and there he'd be, standing over me and growling low. So it was best to stay on my feet and keep my distance. Which was what I was doing when a door opened somewhere nearby, followed by hard footsteps, and then Mr. Immler was standing outside the bars, with Sheriff Hunzinger beside him.

Hunzinger gazed at me and nodded. "You got 'im."

"Yup," said Immler. "Now what do you want me to do?"

"About what?"

Immler pointed at me with his chin.

"Your job," said Hunzinger. "Whatever you're supposed to do."

"In a situation like this, I do an evaluation."

"So do it."

"Already did," Immler said. "Had all his shots, no other incidents on his record, disposition placid. Profile like that, I return to owner with a warning."

"Disposition placid? Darn near took my leg off."

Immler opened his mouth, looked like he was about to say something, but did not. I had maybe a bad thought, all about wishing I had in fact taken the sheriff's leg off. Then I remembered the taste of the sheriff's blood, which I actually hadn't liked at all.

"Just you find some reason for keeping him here," Hunzinger said.

"If you say so."

"I say so. Can't assault a sheriff. That's the beginning of the end, right there."

Immler turned to go. "Just one thing I could point out. Legally a dog can't perform an assault."

"Why the heck not?" said the sheriff.

"Because assault's a human thing," Immler said. "Like what Matty Comeau supposedly did to you."

The sheriff stared at Immler. " 'Supposedly'?"

"Wrong word. My bad. I'll try and come up with something."

"That'd be wise of you," Hunzinger said.

Immler went away. The sheriff stayed where he was, his eyes now on me.

"How's life treatin' you now?" he said.

I didn't know the answer to that question, but I did realize that my tail was drooping. I hoisted it back up, as high as it would go. I didn't want this man to see me with a droopy tail.

He noticed Drogan, over in the back corner, and grinned. "Hey, you, tough guy—why don't you sic 'im?"

Drogan shrank back, surprising me.

Hunzinger shook his head. "Why do people even like dogs? I just don't get—"

He went silent at the sound of more footsteps. Then another man appeared, a large man with a barrel of an upper body and sticklike legs. The sheriff looked at him in surprise.

"Mr. Mahovlich? What are you doing here?"

"Tracking you down, is what. Didn't realize dogcatching was one of your duties."

"The safety of all our citizens is my duty."

"Knock it off, Hunzinger," said this new dude, Mr. Mahovlich. I knew Foster Mahovlich, of course, from hockey, and was hoping that might lead to some helpful thought, but it didn't. "What can you tell me about this murder case?"

"It's an active investigation," the sheriff said.

"I get that. I'm asking where it stands. What have you found out?"

"I can't really go into the details."

Mr. Mahovlich leaned forward, poked Hunzinger's chest with his finger. Then he spoke in a low and sort of buzzing voice, very unpleasant, in my opinion.

"Do you like being sheriff, Hunzinger?"

Hunzinger nodded.

"Want to be sheriff again? When the next election rolls around?"

Hunzinger nodded.

"Good," said Mr. Mahovlich, his voice returning to normal. "We're on the same page. Now what were you saying about the investigation?"

"Right now we got a suspect on the run. We expect to apprehend him very soon."

"Matty Comeau? Why would Matty Comeau kill this guy?"

Mr. Mahovlich was making sense. Of course Matty wouldn't kill whoever it was they were talking about—or anybody, for that matter. He was the gentlest patter in mountain country. Right about then was when I decided that Mr. Mahovlich was a possible friend. I moved as close as possible to him and stuck my head through the bars. Then he'd notice me and say, "Might as well take this pooch with me and drop him off at the Blackberry Hill Inn." I waited.

Meanwhile the sheriff was saying, "Looks like artifacts as the motive."

"What are you talking about?"

"Colonial artifacts. Trading post on the old Sokoki Trail."

"That was a real thing?" said Mr. Mahovlich.

The sheriff shrugged. "Above my pay grade. Point is some people think so—this LeMaire guy had a shovel with him. And Matty's an archaeologist of some sort, doesn't take kindly to random folks digging up the forest."

Uh-oh. Something about Matty and poor Mr. LeMaire? I took a stab at putting things together, but they wouldn't come together.

Mr. Mahovlich had gone still. "A shovel?" he said.

"One of those piddly fold-up numbers, but still," said the sheriff. "And he had a gun on him, too, like he was expecting trouble. Never fired it, since the blow came from behind. Matty musta snuck up on him, quiet-like. He's a primo woodsman, no takin' that away from him. So that's it—open and shut, far as I'm concerned. All that's left is findin' him and bringin' him in."

"Any sign that the shovel got used?" Mr. Mahovlich said.

"Like how?" said the sheriff.

"Holes that got dug up. That would be one clue."

"Carstairs didn't mention any holes."

"But what about you? What did you see?"

"I wasn't up there myself, in actual fact," the sheriff said.

"Ah."

"Bum knee."

Mr. Mahovlich gazed down at the sheriff. The sheriff looked away. Mr. Mahovlich's phone beeped. He glanced at the screen, put the phone away. "One more thing. Has a postcard turned up in your investigation?"

"Postcard? Nope. What kind of postcard?"

"An old one."

"Haven't found anything like that." Hunzinger shot Mr. Mahovlich a quick look. "What's a postcard got to do with anything?"

"Probably nothing. I'm just spinning my wheels."

The sheriff's forehead got all wrinkly. "I don't get it. Do you know something I don't?"

Mr. Mahovlich laughed. "Ha-ha. That's a good one." He patted Hunzinger on the back. "Keep me in the loop, Sheriff." And he walked away, down the cement corridor and out a door I couldn't see. A moment or two later the sheriff went off the same way. Then I was back to being alone with Drogan. I heard him stirring behind me, back in his shadowy corner of our very small room.

FOURTEEN

QUEENIE

THERE SEEMED TO BE A LOT OF problems going on at the Blackberry Hill Inn. Problems disturb my way of life. There are things you can do to block out being disturbed. For example, at the moment, I was sitting on top of the old grandfather clock in the front hall watching myself in the mirror behind the desk. What a nice sight! And so calming! I'd never fully appreciated how beautiful I looked in a sitting position. You learn something every day, as Bertha says. I spent a pleasant time learning everything there was to learn about this exciting development on the subject of me, at first not even hearing the sizzle of something going on in the kitchen. Normally a sound like that is followed almost immediately by the appearance of a certain party, his oversized muzzle sniffing the air. That's a sight that always makes me think, *Oh, not again. Give it a rest.*

But right now I missed it. Despite how much I had going on upstairs—which was plenty, as you must know by now—I couldn't figure out why. And now my way of life was disturbed again. What if I shifted slightly to the side to see myself from a new angle, sort of looking over my shoulder? That sounded really cute, and I was just about to give it a whirl when the front door opened and in came Mr. Mahovlich. With him was a kid who looked to be about Bro's age, although a lot bigger.

"Hello?" said Mr. Mahovlich. "Anybody here?"

What a question! There was me, for instance, so close I could have easily leaped down and landed right on his head. I actually considered it. Then Bertha came in from the kitchen, wiping her hands on her apron. She stopped short when she saw who the visitors were.

"Mr. Mahovlich?" she said. "Foster?"

So this was Foster. I'd heard about him, of course, but this was my first sighting. I examined his nose, and found to my disappointment that even though Bro had popped that nose a good one, it looked quite straight—although in no way pleasing to the eye.

Mr. Mahovlich flashed Bertha a great big smile. "Bertha, isn't it?"

"Correct," said Bertha. "What can I do for you?"

Mr. Mahovlich gave Foster a little push forward. "Foster here has something to say to Harmony."

"Happy to pass it on," Bertha said.

"Well, it's like—" Foster began, but Mr. Mahovlich cut him off.

"He wants to say it in person."

Bertha gave Mr. Mahovlich a long look and said, "I'll see if she's in." Bertha went through the doorway that led to the private part of the house, the clumping of her clogs fading on the stairs.

Then came the unexpected. Mr. Mahovlich said, "Stay put," and hurried to the desk, not stopping in front as visitors were supposed to, but striding around to the back.

"Dad?"

And once he was behind the desk, in what's really the office here at the inn, Mr. Mahovlich began opening drawers and rooting around inside.

"Dad? What are you doing?"

Without looking up, Mr. Mahovlich said, "Shut your mouth." He rooted around some more, then paused and cocked his head to one side. Did he hear those approaching footsteps? I did—goes without mentioning—but Mr. Mahovlich's reaction was pretty quick for human ears. He closed the last drawer, slipped around the desk, and stood by Foster. "Just taking care of business," he said.

"What kind of business?" said Foster.

Mr. Mahovlich put that big smile back on his face as Bertha appeared in the Big Room, now with Harmony beside her. At the same time, he draped his arm over Foster's shoulders, and gave one of those shoulders a hard squeeze. I knew it was hard from how it made Foster wince. "Nothing to worry about," he said in a voice that sounded gentle on the outside.

"Excuse me?" said Bertha as she and Harmony came into the hall.

"Just telling Foster here that there was nothing to worry about. I'm sure Harmony will handle this the right way."

"Handle what?" said Bertha.

Mr. Mahovlich gave Foster another one of those little pushes.

"Uh," Foster said. "Harmony?"

"Yeah?"

"That, like, hip check thing?"

"It wasn't a hip check," Harmony said. "It was boarding."

"Whatever," Foster said. "What I mean is—it won't happen again."

"Louder," said Mr. Mahovlich.

Foster said it again, louder.

"No probs," said Harmony. "We're square."

"Great sportsmanship!" said Mr. Mahovlich. "Or should I say sportspersonship?" He found that last part very funny. It made him laugh and laugh. "Now that's out of the way, I'll be hitting the road. But Foster here was wondering if he could stay and hang out with Bro for a bit."

"Are they back yet?" Bertha said.

"Still at the lawyer's," Harmony said.

"Lawyer's?" said Mr. Mahovlich. "I hope everything's all right."

"It most certainly is not," Bertha said. "That fool sheriff of yours has gone and—"

"Whoa!" Mr. Mahovlich raised his hand. "Whoa there, Ms. Bertha! Whatever in the world makes you think Mr. Hunzinger is my sheriff? He's all of our sheriff, duly elected by the citizens of the county."

"Right," said Bertha.

"But let's not argue politics. Instead how about you fill me in on this problem, whatever it is?"

"Why would I do that?" Bertha said.

"Know how to keep your mouth shut, huh? I admire that. If you ever happen to be in the job market, look me up. And since you're not going to spill the beans, how about I take a guess? This visit to the lawyer is all about a dog bite."

Bertha blew air through her closed lips, one of the better human tricks; it makes a flappy sound that's always nice to hear. "Bite? Barely a scratch, if that."

"Are you saying the sheriff overreacted?"

"That's putting it mildly. We've got a fraidycat for a sheriff."

Oh, dear. Some human expressions make no sense. Fraidycat was one of them, maybe least sensible of all. And to hear it from Bertha, practically a member of the family? I was shocked.

"I wouldn't go that far," Mr. Mahovlich was saying. "But tell you what. I'll look into this, see if I can lower the temperature a little bit."

"What do you mean by that?" Bertha said.

Mr. Mahovlich started in on an explanation. I paid no attention. Some human conversations go on and on, plus the whole fraidycat thing had put me in a bad mood. There's a scratching post in the screened-in porch on the second floor that I sometimes take out my bad moods on, but it was winter, meaning the door to the screened-in porch was locked. Therefore I went the other way, down to the furnace room in search of mice. Even one single mouse would probably do.

It was quiet and dark in the old part of the basement, and I was part of that quietness and darkness in a way I doubt humans can ever be. I made my way around the old furnace and up the coal chute, where that fattish mouse and I had enjoyed a little sport not long ago. No sign of my old buddy now. I went up to the windowsill and gazed through the broken windowpane. The last time I'd taken in this view, snow had been falling and Harmony and Bro were coming across the meadow, trailed by a certain party, waddling his way home. How ridiculous he'd looked! Now there was no one to be seen and the sky was clear and the meadow white.

Arthur. What use was he to anyone? And where was he now? I wasn't at all clear on that. What would happen to someone like him if he got into a ticklish situation? I don't mean actually being tickled. He loves that, wriggles around the floor on his back in a way that's just about unbearable to watch. Wherever he was, I doubted he was being tickled, or enjoying any of his various amusements, each one dumber than the last. The next thing I knew, I was easing myself through the broken windowpane, the jagged glass brushing through the fur on my back like a very sharp comb. Why? For Arthur? What a strange thought! But no other reason came to mind.

Presto! I was out in the world. I knew one thing right away: It had been way too long. I smelled the air, full of lovely outdoor smells, although none of them originated with Arthur. Was he with that dreadful man, Mr. Immler? I realized that finding Arthur was going to mean leaving the property. Fine with me. I hadn't actually been off the property since summer. What an eventful time I'd had! If way too short. I recalled the ride back with Mom, and how she'd turned to me—I like to lie on the back shelf when I'm in her car—and said, "I know you're just following your instincts, Queenie, but I wish you'd put a lid on it." My takeaway from that had been that Mom still loved me, maybe more than ever. But I hadn't been off the property since.

Ah, to be free! My bad mood started to lift and an idea came immediately. I decided to visit Willard's General Store, partly because I knew the way, and partly because humans loved the sticky buns they sold at Willard's and Mr. Immler was a human, although on the low end of the scale. I took a few silent steps in the cool snow, opening up the view beyond the breakfast nook. Meaning I couldn't help but spot the bird feeder.

For some reason or other, the sight of the bird feeder made me go still, one of my front paws poised in elegant fashion. What a lovely picture that must have been, seen from one of the windows of the inn, for example. I hoped nothing like that was actually going on at the moment. *Best to move on, Queenie,* I thought to myself, but just as I did, a tiny red flutter in the big blue sky caught my attention, a tiny red flutter that grew bigger and took winged shape. In short, a cardinal. My bad mood flew away just like that—and at the very moment the bird flew in. How interesting! Was I about to make some amazing mental discovery about moods and flight?

No time for that now. The bird—the only redness in the whole great outdoors, at least my part of it—landed on a little dowel Elrod had so thoughtfully placed before the opening to the birdseed, giving any hungry birdie a place to stand. By the time my cardinal friend touched down, I was already close by, concealed by one of Mom's flowerpots on the patio. From this particular flowerpot to the dowel on the bird feeder is a matter of two little springs to gather momentum and then one mighty leap, front paws at full extension.

None of that happens willy-nilly, by the way, in case you're planning something along the same lines yourself. You have to be patient. Being patient means waiting until your bird stops checking out what's around and gets its tiny mind going on the birdseed. When it finally sticks its head in is actually not the signal to go, not that first time. That first time is almost always a fake, as it was with my cardinal—and what a beauty, by the way! And a he, the bright-red ones being hes and the dull-red ones being shes, as I'd heard Harmony explain to Bro, although he'd shown no signs of listening.

So here came the fake—the head darting into the feeder but then quickly out again, those piercing birdie eyes on the lookout for losers who move too soon. I'm not one of those losers—or any sort of loser. I waited. After not too long—you never have to wait too long with birds, their lives winging by at a brisk pace, which you know for sure the first time you've got one between your teeth and feel that minuscule heart going a mile a—well, maybe too much information. Back to me waiting and the cardinal sticking his head into the feeder once more. The head stayed in longer this time, but it was still a fake, the bird suddenly turning and getting all watchful again. The third time was what I was looking for. I waited.

The cardinal finally made up his mind. I could see it happening. He stepped forward on the dowel, turned toward the opening in the bird feeder, and—

Bang! A window in the breakfast nook got opened in a forceful way. Harmony yelled, "Queenie! What do you think you're doing?"

And my cardinal soared off into the sky, the breeze from his beating wings ruffling my whiskers. Meanwhile Harmony was giving me a look. This was a difficult situation. But here's something about me—one more good something, if I can put it that way. In difficult situations I can keep my poise. I slowly sat down on the patio, taking what I assumed was a graceful position.

"You just wait right there," Harmony called. "Don't move an inch."

Fine with me. The window closed with a thump. A patch of snow slid off the roof and landed with a plop. I waited. I didn't move an inch. I didn't have to wait, of course, and I could have moved much farther than an inch, but I did not. I was being nice.

The side door of the house opened and Harmony appeared, dressed for the outdoors. "Back soon," she said over her shoulder, and came my way. And what a nice surprise! She was carrying my backpack.

"We're going for a walk, you little devil," she said, *little devil* being one of her cute nicknames for me. She set the backpack down, unzipped the see-through mesh part, and said, "In. Be good. This is about Matty, not you."

Not about me? What an odd remark! But I hopped in anyway. So cozy inside the backpack. Harmony zipped up the mesh and hoisted me onto her front, which was how I liked to ride in the backpack. And then we were on the move, around the house and onto the road. One way led to Willard's, the other toward the center of town. That was the direction we took. Lovely day for a walk, the air crisp but still, a car or two passing by, a squirrel in someone's yard. I paid that squirrel no attention.

"What gets into you?" Harmony said.

Ah. So it was about me after all. I considered Harmony's question—the answer had to be something good—as we crossed the village green and came to a small stone building.

"The library," Harmony said. "Bertha says that Mrs. Hale likes cats. Get the picture?"

Certainly. Mrs. Hale, whoever she happened to be, was going to love me.

We entered the library, a place filled with all sorts of musty smells, woody and papery. Plus mouse smell and plenty of it. I filed that away for some future visit to the library, an on-my-own type of visit.

As for people, there was only one, an old woman behind a desk. She wore glasses, had snow-white hair piled high on her head and somehow frozen in place, and wore cardinal-colored lipstick. But getting past all those distractions, there was something very nice-looking about her. Not in a soft way, though. That would have been a mistaken notion. Better to make no mistakes when sizing up humans.

The old woman raised her head. "All backpacks must be checked at the desk," she said. "Rule number one."

"Okay," Harmony said, "but—"

The old woman's eyes narrowed. "Is that a cat in there?"

"Yes, ma'am," said Harmony.

"A cat in a backpack?"

"A special backpack just for cats," Harmony said. "Her name's Queenie and she loves the backpack."

"No pets," said the old woman. "Rule number two."

"Oh, well, maybe I'll leave the backpack just outside the—"

"Queenie, you say?"

149

"Yes."

"Fine name for a cat. Who gave it to her?"

"Actually, it was me," Harmony said. "My name's—"

"I know who you are."

"You do? But I've never set foot here."

"Exactly," said the old woman. "What sort of cat is Queenie?"

"Well, she's very smart," Harmony said.

"What would happen if we let her out of the bag?"

Harmony was silent for a moment. Then she laughed. Did a tiny smile flash on the old woman's face? I thought I caught it. As for what was funny, I was a bit puzzled.

"She'll be good," Harmony said.

"Then ring freedom's bell!"

No bell rang, which was welcome news: The sound couldn't be more irritating. Harmony placed the backpack on the desk and unzipped the mesh cover. I stepped out.

"Ah," the old woman said, "a twenty-four-carat beauty."

What a nice thing to say, even if carrots did nothing for me. I glided across the desk and straight onto the old woman's lap.

"Well, well," she said, and stroked my back. And she was good at it, very close to being in Matty's league. I wondered about organizing a competition between them.

"Are you Mrs. Hale?" Harmony said.

"Correct," said Mrs. Hale, still stroking me. "What can I do for you, Harmony?"

"Well," Harmony said. "It's about Mr. LeMaire. I was wondering about his visit here to the library."

"Why is that?"

"Because the stupid—because the sheriff thinks Matty Comeau is the murderer."

"So I heard."

"But Matty would never do something like that! And I was thinking that maybe Mr. LeMaire left some clues."

"What kind of clues?"

"Clues that would lead to the real killer."

Mrs. Hale's hand came to rest. She gave Harmony a long look. "Any thoughts on what you'd like to be when you grow up?" she asked.

Harmony looked surprised. "No."

"Is there anything you're passionate about?"

"Hockey."

Hockey? I hoped there wasn't going to be much discussion about hockey. What I wanted was more stroking. I considered digging my claws into Mrs. Hale's arm, just very lightly, to send the message, and decided against it.

"But right now," Harmony went on, "I—"

"Right now you'd like to pick my brain," said Mrs. Hale, and she resumed stroking me, so we were back on course.

"All I can tell you is what I told the sheriff. This LeMaire character wanted to know all about the old Sokoki Trail."

"Like what?"

"If I knew of any digging that had gone on up there, for one thing, which I did not."

"He was looking for artifacts?"

"That's what I assumed, and what I told the sheriff." Mrs. Hale's hand went still again. "Although, come to think of it, he never actually mentioned artifacts himself. Just the digging part. He showed me a map he had of the Mount Misty region—just the trail map from the Park Service—and asked if we had any older maps. I found one in the Historical Society Room and showed it to him and he made a copy."

"An old map?"

"Dated 1930."

"Can I see it?"

"Sure." Mrs. Hale rose, with me in her arms. There was a lot to like about Mrs. Hale. The three of us went into a small, wood-paneled room with some framed maps on the wall and old leather-bound books on the shelves. "It's in the bottom drawer on the left-hand side," said Mrs. Hale.

Harmony knelt and opened the drawer. Her face got puzzled. "I don't see an old map, Mrs. Hale. There's only this." She held up something folded and brightly colored.

"Why, that's just the regular Park Service map," Mrs. Hale said. She carried me over to the drawer and we peered inside. The drawer was empty. "I don't understand."

"Was Mr. LeMaire alone in here?" Harmony said.

"Maybe for a few minutes. Don't tell me he switched the maps."

Harmony nodded.

"But why, if he made a copy?" said Mrs. Hale. Her eyes narrowed. "On second thought, I didn't actually watch him make it—can't see the copier from the main desk." She made an angry sort of grunt. "This means he stole from the library."

"He didn't want anyone to ever see that map again," Harmony said.

Mrs. Hale cocked her head to one side, seemed to be studying Harmony. "I do believe you're right," she said. "And what a nasty thing to do—even if the poor soul is dead. I wonder if the sheriff found it among Mr. LeMaire's effects."

"What are effects?" Harmony said.

"The possessions he left behind."

"Oh," said Harmony.

"I'm going to call him this very minute," Mrs. Hale said.

"Um," said Harmony. "Can't hurt."

Mrs. Hale gave her a funny look, perhaps on the verge of saying something sharp like, "And what do you mean by that, young lady?" Then she glanced down at me and changed her mind. Yes, a cat person for sure.

FIFTEEN

ARTHUR

A BIG PROBLEM WITH DROGAN WAS that whenever we got fed, which didn't seem to happen very often, he gobbled up all the kibble. Not even leaving the smallest taste behind in the bowl for me. Once I tried to push my way in—I was so hungry!—and the next moment, before I knew what was happening, he had me by the throat. That was terrible because when someone has you by the throat, how can you fight back? I tried batting him away with my front paws. He sank his teeth in me until I went still.

Another problem was that Drogan didn't seem to need any sleep. I should get a trophy for sleeping, as Bro once told me. And that would be great. I'd love a trophy one day. Bro tells me things I never hear him telling anyone else. Oh, Bro! Please come and get me out of here! I promise to be a good good boy. I won't ever grab the puck again. Was that why this was happening to me? I'll be better! Please, Bro.

Those were the kind of thoughts I was having as I lay in my corner, as far away as I could get from Drogan's corner, waiting for him to close his eyes so I could close mine. If I fell asleep and he didn't, I'd end up awakening with him standing over me, teeth bared, drooling, and eyes wild like a cornered creature. Why? The cornered one was me! Now, finally, his eyes closed. I kept my own eyes open until I no longer could, maybe not a very long time. The next thing I knew I was feeling Drogan's breath on my face.

I snapped my eyes open real fast, my heart waking up, too, if that makes any sense, pounding away like crazy. I wriggled backward, bumping up against the wall right away. All the other times this had happened—these horrible wake-up calls—Drogan just stood there for a while and then slunk off to his corner, like he'd played a fun game and then tired of it. But this time was different. Without warning and with shocking speed, he flipped me over and got me by the neck again. I squirmed and batted, but it did no good. Drogan's teeth pressed harder—slowly, like he was taking his time. But it still hurt.

Then came sounds out in the corridor, human steps and human voices. Drogan's sharply pointed ears went straight up. He let me go and backed away. Drogan was lying in his corner when two men appeared at the bars.

I knew both of these men, Mr. Mahovlich and Sheriff

Hunzinger. Mr. Mahovlich held a bouquet of flowers. He and the sheriff gazed down at me.

"One ugly mutt," the sheriff said.

"Beauty is in the eye of the beholder," said Mr. Mahovlich.

"Never understood that expression."

I was with the sheriff on that, but not on the ugly mutt part. Harmony always said I was the cutest dog on the planet. I trusted Harmony big-time, and the sheriff not at all.

"Doesn't matter," Mr. Mahovlich was saying. "What matters is getting this smoothed out."

"Getting what smoothed out?" said the sheriff. "We got a biter here, case closed."

Mahovlich turned to him. "What kind of town do we want here, Hunzinger?"

"Not one full of wild beasts," said the sheriff, looking in my direction.

Was he checking to see if I agreed with him? I did, and completely. A town full of wild beasts was the scariest thing I'd ever heard.

"Something the matter, Hunzinger?" Mahovlich said. "Pressure getting to you?"

"What pressure?"

"Having an unsolved murder in your jurisdiction."

"Nothing unsolved about it. Matty Comeau's the perp. Now all we gotta do is bring him in."

"How's that going?"

"Carstairs has a search party up on the mountain. He thinks they've picked up his tracks. We've also looped in the state police and the FBI."

"So we can look forward to a happy ending?"

"And soon."

"Good to hear," Mr. Mahovlich said. "And in that spirit, I know you'll want to deliver this mutt back to Mrs. Reddy, together with these."

He held out the flowers. The sheriff regarded them with a frown, like he didn't know what they were. There are probably things I don't know, but flowers isn't one of them. *They're flowers, Sheriff. What's the matter with you?*

"Why would I want to do that?" the sheriff said.

"To demonstrate your forgiving nature."

"Huh? I don't have a forgiving nature."

"I know that, Hunzinger. You'll have to pretend."

"Why?"

"You'll be doing me a favor," said Mr. Mahovlich. "And when folks do me a favor, they get favors back. As I thought you would have known by now."

The sheriff gazed at Mr. Mahovlich, then looked away. He took the flowers. A few moments after that, Mr. Mahovlich was gone. A car started up outside and drove away.

"Immler?" the sheriff yelled. "Get in here."

157

A door opened nearby and Immler came hurrying down the corridor.

"What's up?" he said.

Hunzinger thrust the flowers into Immler's hands. "Take these over to Mrs. Reddy at the Blackberry Hill Inn. Stat. Along with her dog."

Immler blinked. "Her dog?"

"Nothing wrong with your ears," the sheriff said.

I wasn't so sure about that. Immler's ears were on the small side, even for a human, probably not capable of hearing much.

"I don't get it," he was saying.

"Am I asking you to get it?" said the sheriff.

"I like to know the whys and wherefores."

"Do you also like your job, Immler?"

"Oh, sure, I like it fine."

"And who got you this job?"

"Mainly you, although I'm highly qual—"

The sheriff raised his hand in the stop sign. "There's your whys and wherefores," he said. "Text me when it's done."

The sheriff went away. Immler opened the barred door. "Move, you—" He called me a bad name. I stepped outside and right away had a crazy urge to bite his ankle! Can you believe it? Of course I knew that would have been a mistake. I followed him down the corridor, well within ankle-biting range but doing nothing about it. No sense in spoiling this, a pretty good moment in my life, except for the feeling of Drogan's eyes on my back the whole way, and even out in the parking lot.

SIXTEEN

QUEENIE

WE LEFT THE LIBRARY, HARMONY on her feet, of course, and me in the backpack—worn on Harmony's front, as I've mentioned, because I'd rather see where I'm going than where I've been. On the way out, we met a man going in. He didn't notice us at all. His mind was on something else. There's a special sort of blank face humans have for that. You see it all the time, meaning that wasn't the interesting part of this encounter. The interesting part was that I'd seen this man before, although at some distance. But that red beard of his was hard to miss and hard to forget. This was the man who'd waited in the car at the top of our circular drive, while Ms. Mary A. Jones of 419B Zither Street, Brooklyn, New York—not her real name and not a real place, if I'd been keeping up with the facts—had collected the stuff Mr. LeMaire had left behind, including the postcard. Meaning now we couldn't sell it to Mr. Mahovlich, a shame since our financial situation was not good. And there were other meanings from Ms. Mary A. Jones's visit as well, meanings I might get to at some future time if I felt like it. Right now I just wanted to enjoy the great outdoors. The first thing I always do in the great outdoors is check for birds. And I was just getting started on that when Harmony said, "Oops," pivoted around, and back inside the library we went.

Mrs. Hale sat behind her desk, at her keyboard and typing faster than I'd ever seen anyone type, her red-tipped fingers looking like separate living things, dancers, say, doing a speedy dance. There was no sign of the red-bearded man. Mrs. Hale looked up at us in surprise.

"You're back."

"I just thought of something," Harmony said. "Maybe there's a book about it."

"About what?"

"Whisky."

"You're interested in whisky?"

"Old whisky."

Mrs. Hale gave Harmony a look. "How old?"

"We don't know. We have this old bottle and wondered if it's worth anything. Like to collectors."

"Who is we?"

"Me and my brother." Mrs. Hale gave her some more of that look. "And my mom, too," Harmony added.

"Glad to hear that. What's the name on the bottle?"

"Maple Leaf Gold Canadian rye whisky," Harmony said. Ah, that would be the bottle Mr. LeMaire left behind, if I'd been following things right. Which I always do, by the way, except when I don't bother to follow them at all.

"Come with me." Mrs. Hale rose. We followed her into the main room, filled with rows and rows of books. Without a pause or even looking, she plucked one off a shelf, carried it to a table at the back of the room, and turned the pages. "How about this one?"

Harmony looked at a picture on an open page of the book and leaned closer. "That's it."

"Here's what it says," said Mrs. Hale. " 'Maple Leaf Gold rye whisky was actually made from corn, not rye. It was manufactured in a warehouse outside Montreal, Canada, beginning with the onset of Prohibition in the United States in 1920.' "

"What's Prohibition?" Harmony said.

"When no alcohol was allowed anywhere in the country," said Mrs. Hale. She went back to reading. " 'The company, thought to have been controlled by gangsters, went out of business in 1933 when Prohibition came to an end. Maple Leaf Gold was not sold on the Canadian market. The entire output was intended for American consumption, smuggled into the US, primarily through New

Hampshire and Vermont. Very few bottles have appeared on the collectibles market. One bottle turned up on *Antiques Roadshow* in 2004 and was valued at two hundred and fifty dollars.'" Mrs. Hale looked up. "Not nothing," she said, closing the book.

"But not a fortune," said Harmony.

"People don't stumble on fortunes very often," Mrs. Hale said. "I've never seen it happen myself."

Mrs. Hale led us back down the rows. I happened to look sideways, over the top of a bunch of books on a shelf. On the other side stood the red-bearded man, his eyes— green eyes, not a color you see a lot in human eyes—right on Harmony. This was a bit of a shock, and quite unpleasant. I even wanted to do something about it, but what? We were outside and on the way home before something occurred to me. I could have hissed! Why hadn't I? My hiss is very scary, and that would have been the perfect moment. I came close to thinking that I hadn't done my best. A crazy thought, of course, but the bad mood I'd been in before the walk hovered in my mind again, like a cloud.

When we got home, Mom and Bro were in the front hall, taking off their jackets.

"Not on the floor," Mom said. "On the hook."

Bro picked up his jacket with his foot and flicked it up and onto a wall hook—a very cool move, but no one except me was watching. "How come I had to go?"

"To see a lawyer in action," Mom said.

"Action?" said Bro. "She said she couldn't do squat."

"The lawyer can't help us with Arthur?" Harmony said, letting me out of the backpack. I glided up to my command post on the grandfather clock.

"The sheriff is within his rights, according to the lawyer," Mom said. "But I wanted Bro to meet her because I think he's got the makings of a future lawyer."

"Bro?" said Harmony.

"Me?" said Bro.

"Yes, you."

"Does it mean going to school?"

"Law school," Mom told him. "It takes three years. That's after college, of course."

"Forget it," Bro said.

"No need to decide now," Mom said. Hadn't we just had a conversation something like this with Mrs. Hale? Sometimes the meaning of the human world seemed just out of reach, quite possibly more to them than to me.

Mom turned to Harmony. "You took Queenie for a walk?"

"Yeah," said Harmony. "We went to the library. Strange things are going on, Mom."

"Like what?" Mom said.

The front door opened before Harmony could explain. In the doorway stood that horrible Mr. Immler, holding a bouquet of flowers. Beside him, straining on a leash and his tongue practically hanging down to the floor, was Arthur.

Eyebrows rose: Harmony's, Bro's, Mom's. The three of them looked almost like the same person for a moment.

Immler cleared his throat, then cleared it again.

"You have something to say, Mr. Immler?" said Mom.

"I, uh, well, actually the sheriff has decided not to pursue this particular matter. So here's your animal." He leaned down and unclipped the leash. Click. And at the sound of that click, Arthur took off, possibly not in the direction he'd meant to go, meaning he charged outside, where he raced around in a circle, his ludicrous ears straight back in the wind, before suddenly zooming back into the house and straight into Mom's arms. But not for long. He was much too squirmy, and soon he was charging around again, leaping first into Bro's arms and then into Harmony's arms, and back again, and forth, et cetera. He even came close to leaping into Immler's arms, changing his mind at the very last second. Then he skidded to a stop, trotted back to Immler, and raised his leg, right over Immler's shoe tops. Somehow Mom was there to drag Arthur away in the nick of time, or just about.

"Will there be anything else, Mr. Immler?" Mom said.

"There's these." He handed her the flowers.

"They're from you?"

"No way. I mean, um, not from me personally."

"They're from the sheriff?"

"Yeah."

"I find that hard to believe."

"God's own truth," said Immler, "although I'd say it took some persuading."

"Who from?" Mom said.

Immler was silent for a bit. "Well, guess there's no harm in saying. Why hide a good deed, if you see what I mean? It was Mr. Mahovlich."

Mr. Immler left. Some humans you see once or twice in your life and never again. I hoped he was one of those. Meanwhile Harmony was telling Mom and Bro all about our visit to the library, Mrs. Hale, Mr. LeMaire, maps, Prohibition, smugglers—a complicated tale that had barely held my attention the first time, and now did not at all. What I needed was some me time. I curled up on top of the grandfather clock and lost myself in my own private thoughts.

What a delicious sleep I had! That often happens after an outing. As I awoke and stretched on the grandfather clock,

I thought of the broken windowpane in the old part of the basement, and promised myself there would be more outings in the future. Then I remembered how Harmony had spotted me out by the bird feeder, and decided that most of these outings to come would be taking place at night.

Bottom line: I woke up in a very good mood. As I stretched, I looked down on the front hall, empty now, darkness falling outside. Then the front door opened and a man entered, carrying luggage. How nice! A guest, just what we needed. I was so pleased that I didn't notice at first that this guest was the red-bearded man.

The red-bearded man looked around. He spotted me right away; he had an alertness you don't always see in humans. We exchanged stares. His said: *I know you.* Mine said: *I know you, too, and I don't like you.* He turned to the desk. The leather-bound guest register lay on top. The red-bearded man took another glance around, opened the register, and started flipping through. He stopped, gazed at a page, closed the book. Then he tinkled the little silver bell.

Mom came in from a side door, a kerchief in her hair and a whisk broom in her hand.

"Any rooms available?" the red-bearded man said.

My answer would have been *Scram and don't ever let me see you again.* Mom said, "Certainly. And welcome to the Blackberry Hill Inn. I'm Yvette Reddy, the owner."

"Vincent Smithers," said the red-bearded man. They shook hands. "Have you got anything with a balcony? I like views."

"The Violet Room has a balcony and very nice views of Mount Misty," Mom said.

"Just the ticket," said Smithers, handing Mom his credit card and driver's license.

SEVENTEEN

ARTHUR

HOME AT LAST! SAVED BY THE BELL, even if I didn't recall hearing any bells. And what does saved by the bell even mean? I didn't know and didn't care. That's how happy I was. I ran around. I licked everybody. I peed all over the place. I collapsed, totally exhausted.

The next day Mom and I went to the kids' hockey game. We like to sit in the stands halfway up. At one time we didn't bother with a leash at hockey games, but now for some reason we do, Mom holding her end loosely in her hand. The Tigers—that's us, and I root for the Tigers even though the name could be better—wear gold. The other team was in green. The kids look kind of alike in their helmets and uniforms, but I can always tell Harmony from her long hair flying in the wind behind her, and Bro from the way he moves, the top half of him kind of still but his legs always churning. Up and down the ice they all went, chasing the puck. How much fun was that? I wondered if it might be possible to quietly—

169

"Don't even think about it, Arthur," Mom said. "Sit."

I sat, and forgot whatever I might or might not have been thinking about. Not long after that, Bro lofted a long pass to Harmony, who zoomed around a green player and shot the puck right between the goalie's legs. The kids call that the five hole for reasons unknown to me and always get a kick out of scoring that way. I get a kick out of it myself, and—

"Arthur?"

I was back on my feet? And perhaps straining at the leash a little. I put a lid on anything like that. Meanwhile there was some nice cheering in the stands, although not from Mom. She cheered when other kids did well, but not for Harmony and Bro. For them she just clapped softly, and her face got a little pink. Which was what was happening when Mr. Mahovlich came down the row and said, "Mind if I join you?"

This was a first, and Mom looked surprised, but she said, "Of course not," and squeezed over.

Mr. Mahovlich sat down, the metal bench bending from his weight. He wore a long suede coat with a suede belt tied around the middle. Suede is a material I know and like, and belts are always interesting. Mom's hand tightened around my leash.

"Those kids of yours can fly," Mr. Mahovlich said.

"Thanks," Mom said. "And speaking of thanks, I'm very grateful for whatever you did to get Arthur sent home to us."

"Didn't take much doing," said Mr. Mahovlich. "And I've been tempted to nip the sheriff's ankles more than once myself."

Wow! I hadn't been expecting that. I checked out Mr. Mahovlich's teeth, not bad for a human, but pretty much a non-threat in the biting department. Still, I began to see him in a new way.

We watched the game for a bit. The ref blew the whistle and sent Foster—easy to recognize since he was the biggest player on the ice—to the penalty box. For the briefest moment I caught a flash of anger in Mr. Mahovlich's eyes—which were glued to the ref—but only because, unlike Mom, I happened to be watching him.

His face smoothed out and he laughed. "They should name the penalty box after him," he said, and held out a bag of popcorn for Mom.

"Thank you, no," Mom said. She gave Mr. Mahovlich a direct look. "I really am grateful, Mr. Mahovlich—"

"Bud, please."

"—but I have to ask why."

"Why what, Yvette? Hope you don't mind me calling you that."

"It's fine," Mom said. "But why did you do us such a huge favor?"

"Does there always have to be a reason?"

"I think so."

"How about doing the right thing—is that good enough?"

"Of course," said Mom. "If it's true."

Mr. Mahovlich laughed again, this laugh more real to my ears than the last one. Hard to explain why. Human sounds are complicated: Let's leave it at that.

"Well," said Mr. Mahovlich, "it's at least partly true."

"What's the other part?"

Mr. Mahovlich spread his hands. He wore leather gloves, high-quality leather, very soft—simply the best. Was there some way I could just have one of them? "All right, I confess," he said. "I'm still hoping I can tempt you into selling me that old postcard."

"My goodness," Mom said. "What's so important about it?"

"Thought I explained," said Mr. Mahovlich. "It's an old family memento."

Mom glanced down at me. She patted the top of my head. I love that! More! More! And there was some more, although it's never enough.

"I'd just give it to you now if I had it," she said.

Mr. Mahovlich went still. "You don't have the postcard?"

Mom shook her head. "Turned out to be among the belongings left behind by Mr. LeMaire, the poor man who got killed. The sheriff thinks Matty Comeau did it."

"I heard."

"But that's a crazy idea."

"He shouldn't have run," Mr. Mahovlich said.

"I know, but—"

He interrupted her. "What happened to the belongings?"

"A woman—supposedly sent by Mr. LeMaire, but that was false—came to pick them up. I made a copy of her ID, of course, but it was false, too."

"So she got the postcard?"

Mom nodded.

"Did you happen to see what was written on the back?" Mr. Mahovlich said.

"Isn't the picture on the front the important part?" Mom said. "If it's just a family memento?"

"Sure," said Mr. Mahovlich. "I was just hoping there'd be some . . . details from the old days, you might say, give it some flavor."

"Well, there was a date, I think sometime in 1932," Mom said. "I don't recall who it was sent to or who signed it. I do remember the message—I guess since there wasn't much to remember."

"Oh?"

"It was just the letter *C*. Is there any period flavor in that?"

Mr. Mahovlich got a very bright look in his eyes. "Nope," he said, and turned to the game, just as Foster was stepping out of the penalty box. Harmony, her long hair flying straight back, saw him right away and zipped him the puck. Foster skated in on goal all alone and blasted the puck into the net. Mr. Mahovlich raised his fist. "Yeah!" he shouted, and then, noticing Mom watching him, lowered his hand and said *Yeah* again, much more quietly.

"Good game, kids," said Mom as we walked home, the kids with their sticks and hockey bags, me in the lead.

"Thanks, Mom," Harmony said.

"I played bad," said Bro.

"What are you talking about?" Mom said.

"You had two assists," said Harmony. "Including on the winner."

"I let number nine walk right around me on the goal before that."

"Bro?" said Mom. "Have we been through this before?"

"That thing about sometimes the opponent makes a good play so you just tip your cap and move on?"

"Exactly," said Mom.

That seemed to satisfy Bro, although I didn't see why. There were no caps in hockey, unless helmets were caps. I was puzzling over that when Harmony said, "I saw you sitting with Mr. Mahovlich."

"He's still interested in that postcard," said Mom.

"How come?" said Harmony.

"Family memento."

We walked on in silence. After a while Bro said, "One thing about the murder."

"What's that?" said Mom.

"I'm talking about the murder of Mr. LeMaire."

"It's the only one we've got," said Harmony.

"Thankfully," said Mom. "Go on, Bro."

"Well, it wasn't, like, random. You know. Two guys meeting in the woods and getting into a fight. Because whoever did it must have had a plan . . . um, in place. To send that woman to pick up the stuff. All that."

Mom and Harmony stopped, gazed at Bro. I stopped because they stopped, I hoped not for long. Hockey makes me hungry.

"Hey," said Mom.

"Bro?" said Harmony. "You're saying the woman did it?"

"It's a thought," said Bro.

"Bro!" Mom said.

"What?" said Bro.

"Nothing," said Mom.

"You must have meant some—" Bro began, but we got interrupted by sirens. Moments later a bunch of police cruisers shot past. Deputy Carstairs was driving the lead car. In the back of the last car, screened off from the front seat, sat Matty Comeau, his face all bloody.

EIGHTEEN

QUEENIE

I WAS ALL ALONE AT THE BLACKBERRY Hill Inn. I don't mind being alone. In fact, I often prefer it. Not that I don't care for Harmony, Bro, and Mom. But sometimes it's nice to simply curl up in a patch of sunshine and think interesting thoughts. About birds, for example. And I was doing just that on the rug in the small parlor where we had the honor-system bar and that noisy table game—foosball, I believe it's called—when I heard the tread of a moving human up above and remembered that I was not quite alone. We had a guest, namely Vincent Smithers, the red-bearded man. I changed my position, curling up in a slightly different way, and guided my mind back to the exciting world of birds. But my mind did not want to stay there, instead wanted to worry about the man upstairs. That was annoying. When I'm annoyed I like to do something about it. Hunting mice in the basement was one option. Chewing something to bits—specifically something that belonged to Vincent Smithers—was another. I chose that one and went upstairs.

I made my silent way past all the empty guest rooms to the Violet Room at the end. Mr. LeMaire's old room, but now Vincent Smithers had it. That was interesting. I could hear him moving around inside. The door was closed, not even open a crack, which is all I need. Fully closed doors are a problem. Some dogs can manage door handles. I've seen it on TV. I'd been sitting on Bro's lap at the time. He'd begun training Arthur to open doors that very moment and had continued the training for many days. In the end, Arthur had scored many treats, some of which—deer antlers, for example—had gotten him going like you wouldn't believe, but he hadn't learned even the very first thing about opening doors.

I listened to Smithers moving around in the Violet Room. He grunted a few times and once said a bad word. I picked up his smell, somewhat garlicky—not uncommon with humans—mixed with stale armpit sweat, also not uncommon. I can smell and hear in ways you can't—it's another kind of seeing—but sometimes you just have to see with your eyes. I turned and trotted into the next guest room— the Daffodil Room, all yellow and my favorite, although that wasn't my reason for entering. My reason was that the Daffodil Room and the Violet Room share a bathroom. The door from the Daffodil Room to the bathroom was open a crack, no problem for me, as you already know if you've been paying attention. The door from the bathroom to the Violet Room was open slightly more than that, just wide enough for me to stand there and peek through.

Vincent Smithers wore a T-shirt and boxers, not a look that shows some human males—like him, for one—in the best light. But it did reveal the small gun he wore in a holster around his ankle. He had the Violet Room turned upside down: mattress on the floor, sheets scattered, drawers out of the dresser, bureau pulled away from the wall. He'd even taken the back off the TV. I prefer things nice and tidy. I was liking Vincent Smithers less and less all the time.

His phone rang. He picked it up. "Nothing," he said. "Nada. Zip." Someone spoke on the other end. I couldn't make out the words, but I could tell it was a woman, and even knew who: Ms. Mary Jones, although that hadn't turned out to be her real name. Whatever she said didn't please him.

"Why are you such a quitter?" he said. "It's got to be somewhere." He kicked over a wastebasket. Nothing came out. Guest wastebaskets are emptied every morning at the Blackberry Hill Inn. We have standards.

The woman spoke again. Whatever she said caught his attention.

"They got him? That's a lucky break, takes the pressure off."

Mary Jones's voice rose, and now I could make out what she was saying. "Not if he can prove his innocence. Then it does the opposite. Stop all this. Come home."

"Are you crazy?" said Smithers. "We're so close. I can taste it."

"You're the crazy one," Mary Jones said, and she clicked off.

Smithers stood there, his chest heaving like he'd been doing something hard, instead of just talking on the phone. Then his eyes got an inward look. "Can I trust her?" he said softly. "Or will I have to . . ." His voice trailed off. He got down on the floor, peered under the bed. Of course he couldn't trust her: She didn't use her real name! As for what Vincent Smithers was tasting, I had no idea. I myself was tasting a nice leather wallet, which I carried away, back through the Daffodil Room, down the stairs, and into my spot on the rug in the small parlor. I chewed on it contentedly for a while, and then took it to a hard-to-get-to spot in one corner, behind the wine rack, and left it for later. I'm the type who makes plans for the future. At this moment you're probably thinking that Arthur is the opposite type, and you'd be right.

I was at my command post on the grandfather clock when Mom, the kids, the hockey bags and hockey sticks, and

Arthur came through the door, everything and everyone somehow tangled in the leash. Normally that kind of scene leads to laughter and fun in these parts, but now it did not. Mom said, "For god's sake, Arthur." His tail stopped wagging. He rolled over and played dead, but no one was amused or even watching.

Mom's phone rang. She listened, said, "Of course I'll do what I can," and hung up. "That was Matty's mom. She's trying to raise money to hire a fancy lawyer from Boston."

"We're going to help, right?" said Harmony.

Mom took a deep breath. "The truth is we're down to our emergency fund."

"How much is in it?" Harmony said.

Before Mom could answer, Vincent Smithers came down the stairs, dressed for the outdoors. He stopped and glanced around. "Is something the matter?" All at once his eyes got big and liquidy, like he was the caring type.

"Thanks for asking," Mom said. "It's nothing for you to worry about. We just want you to enjoy your stay."

"I am so far," Smithers said. "But at the same time I'd hate to be a burden if you're going through some troubles."

"That's very thoughtful of you," Mom said. "It's not about us, not directly. A relative has been arrested for a crime he didn't commit."

"Not a serious crime, I hope?" said Smithers.

"Murder," Harmony said.

Smithers put his hand to his chest. "Goodness gracious! Murder in a beautiful place like this?"

"So the sheriff says," Mom said. "But anyone who knows Matty—he's the one who got arrested—knows he's not capable of murder. Some of us are trying to raise the fee for a top lawyer."

"Good idea," Smithers said. "Happy to make a contribution."

"Oh, we couldn't accept that," Mom said.

"Just a small one," he said, patting his pockets. "It would be my . . . that's funny. Must have left my wallet in the room. Back in a jiffy." He went upstairs.

"What a nice man!" Mom said.

Mom is very smart and almost always right about everything, but not this. Vincent Smithers was not a nice man. Now I had a big problem: How to let her know? I don't like big problems. I don't like small problems. What I like is peace and quiet and the freedom to pursue my one or two little hobbies. Is that too much to ask? Why is it that my simplest demands can never—

The desk phone rang. It was one of those phones with an irritating ring. And I was already in an irritable mood. And for good reason. None of this was my fault. Imagine

182

what a world we'd have if everyone in it was just like me. What a happy thought! I felt a little better at once.

Meanwhile, Harmony had picked up the phone. "Blackberry Hill Inn. How can I help you?" Which is how she answers the desk phone, different from Bro, who just says "Hey!" or sometimes "Yo."

Harmony listened, said, "Uh, sure. Thanks." And hung up.

"Who was that?" Mom said.

"Mrs. Hale at the library. She might have some more information on the whole map thing. But only if I bring Queenie along."

Then all eyes were on me, up on the grandfather clock. Why couldn't I be left alone? Was that a lot to ask?

"Come on down, Queenie," Harmony said. "Let's go see Mrs. Hale. She likes you."

And I supposed I liked her, too. But I wasn't feeling up to an expedition. I needed some personal time. Therefore I just sat motionless, making not the slightest movement, not even blinking my golden eyes.

"Is she blanking out?" Bro said.

"I don't know," said Mom. "She's hard to read sometimes."

"Maybe," said Harmony. "But she never blanks out." She looked up at me again. "Mrs. Hale's been baking. She has some homemade catnip treats."

Catnip was suddenly in the picture? Why couldn't this have been presented in a more organized manner? I wondered about that as I glided down from the command post and tiptoed—no idea why I did that, just giving in to a sudden inspiration—over to Harmony and arched my back a few times.

"See?" said Harmony.

"Nope," Bro said.

Vincent Smithers came back down. The nice-guy look was still on his face, but his eyes weren't joining in.

"My wallet seems to be missing," he said.

"Oh, dear," said Mom.

"Has anyone seen it? A black leather wallet, like so." He made a shape with his hands. I actually remembered the wallet as being smaller than that, but I could have been wrong.

Meanwhile everyone—everyone but me—was shaking their heads. I kept my own head perfectly still, gazing across the room at my still self in the mirror. It was like . . . like there were two of me. Was there any way to make it three?

"Do you remember when you last had it?" Mom said. "You could try retracing your steps."

Smithers shot Mom an unpleasant look that turned more pleasant in a flash, but I caught it. "Helpful ideas," he said, a muscle bulging in his jaw.

"Bro's good at finding things," Mom said.

"I am?" said Bro.

"And he knows every inch of this place. He'll be happy to help you."

Bro opened his mouth, closed it. He didn't look happy. I love Bro and felt some sympathy, but I was already tuning out the wallet issue. What did it have to do with me, in what humans call the grand scheme of things? In the grand scheme of things, something much more important waited in my future—my very very very near future, I hoped—namely homemade catnip treats. I'd been living in this town for some time, in fact all my life. Why had it taken this long to meet Mrs. Hale?

NINETEEN

ARTHUR

NOTHING SHARPENS THE APPETITE
like hockey, which is how come it's my favorite
game. There's the puck, too, of course—so much
fun for your teeth, or at least mine. Chewing on a baseball
is also lots of fun, don't get me wrong. All the surprising
stuff inside when you get the cover off! We're very involved
in sports, me and the kids.

But back to my appetite. I was so hungry I could have
eaten a horse. Well, not that. Living in mountain country,
I've had some experience with horses, none good. Why are
they so edgy? The first time I got kicked by one of those
hard hooves, I was totally unprepared. And the time after
that, and many other possible times, so now I don't go
anywhere near horses, but just bark at them from a safe
distance. Out the open car window is best.

Where were we? Right, my appetite. What was all
this palaver in the front hall? Something about a missing
wallet? Who was the dude with the red beard? A guest,

maybe? That would be nice, but I couldn't wait for the details. Instead I trotted off toward the kitchen, possibly dragging my leash behind me.

What was going on? No Bertha? Was this her day off? Maybe she was on one of her coffee breaks. I checked my kibble bowl—empty—and went looking for her. But I'd barely left the kitchen when I heard Mom say, "And take Arthur with you. A walk will do him good."

I froze. Another walk? So soon? How much good could I take?

We went outside, me, Bro, and this red-bearded dude, who Bro called Mr. Smithers. Mr. Smithers smelled garlicky—a smell I used to like but don't anymore, not after a sort of tasting adventure I had in the kitchen, shortly after spotting a whole garlic within easy range on the slicing board. But Mr. Smithers also smelled of stale armpit sweat, not a bad smell at all in my book, so I decided there and then that he had to be all right.

"What's your name again?" he said.

"Bro," said Bro.

"As in 'brother'?" said Mr. Smithers.

"I guess so."

"So it's more of a nickname?"

"Everybody calls me Bro."

"Okay, then, Bro. And what's the name of this mutt?"

"Arthur."

Mutt? I'd heard that so many times! I suppose it had to be true. I am a mutt, although what a mutt actually is isn't clear to me. But something less than the best. Maybe I wouldn't be hearing it again. Yes, what a nice thought! I got back to feeling chipper at once.

"Is he any good at finding things?" said Mr. Smithers.

"Oh, yeah," said Bro. "The problem is what he does to them after."

Mr. Smithers's eyes—green, which you don't see every day—seemed to get a bit greener. "What do you mean by that?"

"Uh," Bro said. He glanced around, as though looking for help. "Um. Nothing."

"Go on," Mr. Smithers said. "Sounds like you have something interesting to say."

"Not me," said Bro. "So, it's like a wallet that's missing?"

"Exactly like a wallet," Mr. Smithers said. "Leather. Black. Coach."

"Coach?"

"The maker, inscribed on one corner."

"And you maybe dropped it somewhere out here?" Bro said.

"It's a possibility."

Bro thought about that. "Leather, huh?"

"Correct."

Bro nodded. Then he unzipped his jacket, took off his belt, and held it in front of my nose. "Got it, Arthur?"

As if I needed reminding about the smell of leather. But I loved Bro, and the thought of loving Bro made my tail start wagging. Yes, my tail has thoughts of its own, but no time to go into that now.

"See?" said Bro. "He's got it. Arthur's much smarter than people think."

"I'll take your word for it," Mr. Smithers said.

We started across the circle, all nicely plowed down to the gravel by Elrod. I picked up his scent at once—a very nice mixture of beans and mustard—and also Mr. Smithers's scent, not the one coming from him now, but earlier. I sniffed my way along that earlier scent, a sort of smell path. Always fun to follow a smell path. This one was easy, what with the air still, and maybe cold. I stuck my tongue out, felt the air: yes, cold. The rest of me can't really feel the cold, on account of my coat. Nothing muttish about my coat, amigo! Oops! Mutt again, and just when I thought I'd gotten rid of the idea forever. And I'd brought it up myself. It's a funny world. Meanwhile leather slipped my mind completely. A good thing: You don't want a lot of distractions when you're on a tracking mission. Then

I remembered leather was actually what we were looking for and got a bit confused.

Cold is better than warm for following scents, making them clearer, although explaining how would be impossible so I won't even try. Mr. Smithers's scent led away from the parking lot—a bit of a surprise—and along a crushed-stone path, also nicely plowed by Elrod—that led around the house. When we got to the patio—near the bird feeder, where I'd witnessed a scary scene or two I don't even want to think about—Mr. Smithers's old scent trail, not old old, but more like yesterday, or perhaps last night, took a sharp turn straight to the windows that looked into the breakfast nook. The scent grew stronger, like Mr. Smithers had spent more time there, outside the windows. I wondered why. Looking in, maybe? That was as far as I could take it, actually a bit farther than my normal distance.

"Any chance you lost it around here?" Bro said. He kicked at a clump of frozen leaves that lay on the gravel. There was nothing under them.

"Why do you ask that?" Mr. Smithers said.

"Because—" Bro pointed his chin in my direction. "When Arthur stops and keeps sniffing the ground like that, it usually means . . . you know."

"No, I don't."

"That he's found something."

"Not this time," Mr. Smithers said, his voice sharpening. He flashed Bro a brief half smile, or even less, toned his voice down, and added, "I was never here."

What? I couldn't believe my ears. Although I always believe my ears. The way my believing goes is nose first, ears second, eyes third. Whoa! I forgot tongue. What a mistake! Tongue is for tasting! So it went taste first, then—

"Arthur, come on. You're wasting time."

Wasting time? But weren't we looking for something Mr. Smithers had lost, the actual object escaping me at the moment? So why wouldn't it be here? Mr. Smithers had spent time here, no doubt about it. I'm a big fan of humans in general, but Mr. Smithers was suddenly getting hard to like.

"Arthur! Move it."

"You should use a leash," said Mr. Smithers.

Bro gets a certain look at times that reminds me of me, specifically of me when I'm digging in my heels. Bro had that look now. "Arthur doesn't need a leash," he said.

Bro and me: soul brothers, if I understand what that means exactly, and there's a good chance I don't. For the longest time, I thought that hot dogs had something to do with . . . well, you know, and wouldn't touch them. Now at last I know better, and scarf them up every chance I get, cooked or not.

"Arthur!"

I got my act together, trotted after Bro and Mr. Smithers. Trotted after them and nosed my way into the lead. I like to be first. Mr. Smithers's old scent—was it even important now? Or ever?—led all around the house to the parking lot and right to a big black SUV.

"Your car?" Bro said.

"Yes."

"Maybe you dropped it here."

We looked all around the car, for what I wasn't sure. Then from out of nowhere it hit me: wallet! Wow! I was having a very good day. Wallet would never leave my mind again.

Mr. Smithers got down on his hands and knees and checked underneath the car. Usually the sight of a human on hands and knees gets me excited and I can't wait to mix in, but not this time. The wallet wasn't there, which I already knew, since no wallet smell—not just leather, by the way, but also wafting off hints of human skin, plastic, and paper—was in the air. We circled back to the house, all eyes on the driveway—except for mine, which preferred taking in this view and that—and then returned to the car.

"Anywhere else it could be?" Bro said. "Like inside?"

"Not likely," said Mr. Smithers. "I keep my wallet in my pocket." He unlocked the car anyway and started searching inside—under the seats, in the side pockets and the coffee holders, behind the visors. But not the glove box. An interesting smell came from inside the glove box, although it had nothing to do with wallets. Instead it came from a gun. There's a kind of oil they use on guns, a scent I know well on account of the hunters we get in the fall, a scent you really can't miss.

Mr. Smithers backed out of the car.

"What about the glove box?" Bro said.

"Wouldn't be in there."

"But Arthur is kind of sniffing at it."

"Smart pooch," said Mr. Smithers. "Is he a fan of peanut butter and jam sandwiches?"

"Probably."

Mr. Smithers laughed and gave me a pat, at the same time kind of pushing me away from the glove box. But sort of making it look like a pat, if you see what I mean. I got a bit puzzled. The next thing I knew we were all standing outside the car and the doors were closed. What had gone on? My only idea was about PB&J, of which there was none anywhere near here. I did remember coming across a leftover PB&J sandwich up on Mount Misty, the day before Harmony and I found the poor Mr. LeMaire. In fact, I could almost taste it. Wouldn't a PB&J sandwich be perfect right about now? Nothing like that seemed to be in the cards. I had what struck me as an important thought: Why not? Why no PB&J when you needed it?

"So," Bro said, "where else?"

Mr. Smithers glanced back at the house. "Is theft ever a problem around here?"

"What do you mean?"

"Theft. Someone stealing from the guest rooms."

"Never," said Bro. "Besides, you're the only guest right now."

"That doesn't rule out . . ." Mr. Smithers stopped himself and began again. "I'm sure you're honest people." He reached into his pocket. "Here's twenty bucks. Thanks for the help."

Bro made no move to take it. "I didn't do anything."

"Hey, kid. Twenty bucks is twenty bucks."

That sounded right to me. But not to Bro. He wouldn't take the money.

Mr. Smithers seemed to relax a little. He leaned against the car. The sun came out from behind a cloud and warmed things up, also turned Mr. Smithers's beard a brighter red. He looked around. "Beautiful country," he said. "You must like living here."

Bro shrugged.

"Play any sports?"

"Hockey."

"Fastest game going," said Mr. Smithers.

"You play?" Bro said, sounding interested in Mr. Smithers for the first time.

"Nope. But I'm buddies with a couple of the Rangers."

"Yeah?"

"Khovlev and Ricci. I could probably get them to sign a puck or two, ship them up here for you."

"Really?"

"You'd like that?"

"Oh, yeah." Pucks were coming? Great news! Had I been on the verge of disliking Mr. Smithers? I couldn't think why.

"Consider it done," he said. Then he looked again to the mountains and pointed. "What's that one?"

"Mount Misty."

Mr. Smithers gazed at it for a while. "Worried about your relative?"

"Matty?" said Bro. "Yeah."

"What's he like?"

"Matty's the coolest guy. He taught us to skate, me and my sister. Best hockey player ever in this town and he woulda gone pro like your buddies, except for those concussions."

His eyes still on Mount Misty, Mr. Smithers said, "Your father didn't teach you to skate?"

Bro looked down. "Nope."

"Interesting." Mr. Smithers turned to Bro. "But as for your friend Matty, wasn't he up there when the body got found?"

"Just doing his job."

"Your sister was the one who actually discovered the guy?"

"Yeah."

"What was his name again?"

"Mr. LeMaire."

"Any idea what he did?"

"Like, uh . . ."

"For a living."

"Nope," Bro said. "Well, maybe something about liquor."

Mr. Smithers went still. "Yeah? What makes you say that?"

"It's kind of complicated."

"You're a smart kid. I bet you can paint me a picture."

"Of what?"

Mr. Smithers waved his hand at Mount Misty. "This whole thing. I might be able to help your friend."

"Yeah?"

"I'm a troubleshooter by trade."

"What's that?"

"Someone who solves tough problems," said Mr. Smithers. "But I can't do that without having all the facts."

"Like what?" said Bro.

The front door of the inn opened and Mom looked out. She saw us, cupped her hand to her mouth, and called, "Any luck?"

"Not so far," Mr. Smithers called back.

"Bro? I need you to go on back to the woodpile and split some logs. We're getting low."

"Soon," called Bro.

"Now."

TWENTY

QUEENIE

I DON'T GET OUT ENOUGH. I'D EVEN forgotten how much I enjoy it. Out on my own at night is the best, but riding in my backpack with Harmony is a close second. All the sights pass by at just the right speed to entertain me. What a pretty town I had! Although I wasn't an expert on the layout, probably on account of the not-getting-out-enough issue. For example, I'd never realized that Emma Carstairs's house actually faced the village green, not more than a few steps from the library. And there was Emma out front, sticking a carrot nose into the head of a snowman in her yard. A very unusual feeling came over me, close to a wish that Arthur were here. He lifts his leg against every snowman he sees, which is quite a large number when winter really gets going in these parts.

"Hey!" said Harmony. "Cool snowman."

"Hi, Harm," Emma said. "He needs a name."

We went closer. I like Emma, partly because of her pigtails, partly because she has a voice that reminds me of cream—don't ask me to explain—but mostly because she's a big fan of me.

She gave me an admiring look. "Queenie looks so funny in that thing."

"I know, but she loves it," said Harmony.

Funny is one of those words with many meanings. In this case it meant adorable.

Harmony gazed at the snowman. "How about Señor Blizzardo?"

Emma laughed. Señor Blizzardo must have been a joke of some sort, and a good one, because Emma laughed and laughed. Then, without warning, she was crying instead.

"Emma? What's wrong?"

"I'm going to miss you."

"Miss me? What are you talking about?"

"If I live with my mom. She's moving to Boston, can't stand it here anymore."

Harmony hugged Emma, but not too close, what with me jammed in between them. Emma's tears landed on my head. I hate getting wet but decided to be a good sport, at least for a moment or two.

"Can't you stay here with your dad?" Harmony said.

"I don't know. He's even more upset than she is. My dad's kind of out of his mind these days."

"That explains a lot," Harmony said.

Emma went still and her tears dried up. "What do you mean?"

"Nothing. Sorry. Didn't mean anything."

Emma stepped back. Her face was all pink and splotchy. "Yes, you did."

Harmony shrugged. "It's just about Matty Comeau, my cousin. The sheriff's messing up the case and your dad's too wea—and your dad's not stopping him. Now I under—"

"Because he's weak? Is that what you were going to say?"

Harmony nodded.

Emma burst into tears, ran into her house—a small, pretty yellow house with green shutters—and slammed the door. We hurried after her and knocked.

"Emma? Emma?"

But she didn't answer or come to the door. We turned away. The clouds had darkened and the whole town looked black and white, except for Señor Blizzardo's carrot nose.

"These are what I call catnip nipnips," Mrs. Hale said. "My own recipe. Let's see if Queenie likes them."

We were in the library, sitting at Mrs. Hale's desk—Mrs. Hale in the big chair, Harmony in the little chair, and me actually on the desk. Mrs. Hale took out a baggie and from it produced a small tubular treat, about the size of a Cheeto, but far more interesting. She laid it on the desk. All eyes were then on me.

Catnip. I smelled it right away, of course, and the impulsive side of me was suddenly the only side. Normally, as I'm sure you know by now, I'm the dignified type, delicate in my responses, the very farthest thing from greedy. And the truth is, I prefer to eat in private. I suppose I could have taken my catnip nipnip—what a fine name!—under the desk, but by the time that thought came to me, it was all gone.

"Wow, that was quick," Harmony said.

And there was some back and forth between her and Mrs. Hale about the catnip nipnip and me and speediness, but I was unable to pay attention. There was only one thing in my mind: *more!* Well, two things, really, the other one being: *now!*

More!

Now!

More!

Now!

"Maybe she wants another one," Harmony said.

"Hard to tell with her sitting so still like that," said Mrs. Hale.

"But her eyes are on fire."

"I noticed that." Mrs. Hale opened her baggie and slid another catnip nipnip across the desk in my direction. I extended a paw toward it, the movement slow and graceful, almost a kind of dance between me and the nipnip. And then, in a flash, there was only one dancer left onstage.

"Wow!" said Harmony.

"Safe to say she likes them," said Mrs. Hale as she— what was this? Put the baggie away in a drawer?

More!

Now!

More!

Now!

"What's the name of your cat, Mrs. Hale?" Harmony said; or something of the sort. My eyes may or may not have been on fire, but my mind most certainly was.

"I don't have a cat at the moment," Mrs. Hale said. "If anyone can be said to have a cat. The reality is that they have us."

More!

Now!

Mo—

Say again? We the cats have them the humans? Despite the don't-mess-with-me look in her eyes and those down-turned corners of her mouth, there was a lot to like about Mrs. Hale.

". . . always had cats until two years ago," Mrs. Hale said. "Which was when I remarried. And shortly afterward

Mr. Right became Mr. Wrong. He did the worst thing possible."

"What was that?" Harmony said.

"He developed—allegedly developed—an allergy to cats. Tell me this, Harmony—is that grounds for divorce?"

"It depends," Harmony said.

"Of course it depends, child!" Mrs. Hale smacked her hand on the desk. "But if you had to give a yes or no answer, what would it be? Grounds for divorce, yes or no?"

"No."

Mrs. Hale nodded. "That was the decision I came to myself. But it was this close." She held up her thumb and finger with no space between them. For a moment her eyes got a faraway look; then she gave her head a quick shake and said, "But that's not why I asked you here, Harmony. Partly it was the catnip, but—"

More!

Now!

"—but mostly it was the map. I'm talking about the map that Mr. LeMaire stole from right under my eyes. That map is important, no matter what Sheriff Hunzinger thinks."

"He doesn't think it's important?"

"He doesn't think, period. Well, perhaps I go too far. Who would believe that we could elect any official incapable of thought? Let's just say the sheriff is incapable of logical thought. And what's the sine qua non of crime solving?"

"I'm sorry?"

"What's the one thing a crime solver must be good at?"

"Logical thought?"

"Bingo, young lady!" said Mrs. Hale. "The crime solver pieces together a chain of clues in a logical manner and then . . . what's the expression?"

"I'm not sure."

"Drops the hammer! That's it. The crime solver drops the hammer on the bad guy."

"The sheriff already dropped the hammer on Matty Comeau," Harmony said.

Mrs. Hale waved her hand like she was shooing off flies. "Is there a chance on god's green earth of Matty Comeau killing anybody?"

"That's the whole point!"

"Well, there is one chance—if that map was found in Matty's possession. I called the sheriff and asked about that. He confirmed that Matty did not have the map and I told him to release the prisoner at once."

"You told the sheriff that?"

"Why wouldn't I?"

"Do you know him well?"

"Inside and out. I used to be a schoolteacher, third grade at Ethan Allen Primary. I had the sheriff in my very first year. Worst nose picker I've ever seen, before or since. Of course he didn't release Matty, due to his brainlessness where logic is concerned."

"So the map is part of a logic chain?" Harmony said.

"Exactly! Precisely! On the button! Do you want to be sheriff someday, Harmony?"

"No."

"Don't be hasty."

"I wouldn't want to cuff anybody," Harmony said.

"I sure would," said Mrs. Hale. "Better think that over." Her eyes met mine. We sort of locked gazes. "How splendid," she said.

"Cuffing people?"

"Not that, although come to think of it . . ." Mrs. Hale's voice trailed off. "Where were we?"

"The logic chain."

"Bingo again!" Mrs. Hale said. "One—Mr. LeMaire steals map. Two—therefore map is important. Three—map is important to Person X. Four—Person X kills Mr. LeMaire, takes map. Five—whoever took map is the killer."

Harmony got a very thoughtful look on her face. It went so still and beautiful, and I'm not saying that just because I love her. "Um," she said at last. Not much of a reaction, you might say, but to my ear an "um" full of meaning. As for whoever took the map, that had to be Arthur, if I was remembering right, and why wouldn't I be? Therefore Arthur was the killer. There! Done! Case closed!

"So," Mrs. Hale went on, "what's the first question that comes to mind?"

That was easy: When is that baggie of nipnips coming out of the drawer?

But that wasn't Harmony's answer. Instead she said, "What's so interesting about the map?"

"Yessiree," said Mrs. Hale. "That was the starting point for my research."

"Your research?"

Mrs. Hale leaned forward. "I'm a reference librarian, Harmony. Research is what I do."

"Oh."

"Rule one for research," Mrs. Hale said. "Start at the beginning, begin at the start. With me so far?"

"Actually—"

"Meaning first I had to look into the history of that map. How had it ended up here in the library's possession?"

"The library bought it?" Harmony said.

"My first thought, since most of our books and materials come out of the budget. There was no record of any such map purchase. But sometimes we get donations—often just a box of old books and magazines—and when that happens we sort the wheat from the chaff and—"

"They send wheat?"

"It's just an expression, Harmony. We separate the useful from the useless, junk the useless and catalog the useful. In short, I know where that map came from." Behind her glasses, Mrs. Hale's eyes were gleaming. They looked for a moment like a young person's eyes.

"Where?" said Harmony.

Mrs. Hale rubbed her hands together. That's a human thing for when they're leading up to something, possibly good, although not necessarily—for example, that time when Elrod got the idea that the chain saw could be fixed with duct tape.

"Do you know any of the Pelter family?" Mrs. Hale said.

"No."

"Perhaps not. There used to be a lot of them around here. Some families peter out and others go on forever. Any idea why that is?"

Harmony shook her head. "But I hope mine is the second kind."

"That will be partly up to you," said Mrs. Hale. "Let's not worry about it now. The key fact is that when old Thurston Pelter went into assisted living some ten years ago, his books got boxed up and sent to us. And in one of those boxes, according to our records, was a map we labeled 'Hand-Drawn Local Trail Map, circa 1925–1935' and placed in that drawer in the map room. Where it remained until Mr. LeMaire came along. What do you think of that?"

"Maybe old Thurston Pelter knew something about the map?"

"My thought exactly! So imagine my delight when I discovered that old Thurston Pelter is even older now."

"He's still alive?"

"One hundred and one, as of last July." Mrs. Hale rose and picked up her purse, and snapped it shut. "How about you and I pay him a visit?"

"Now?"

"When would be better?" Mrs. Hale said.

Harmony jumped up, then paused and glanced at me. "What about Queenie?"

"They'll love her at Evergreen House," said Mrs. Hale.

I got zipped into my backpack and loaded up onto Harmony's front. My eyes were on that drawer of Mrs. Hale's desk the whole time until we were actually out the door. I didn't care about Evergreen House, whatever that was, or whatever the people inside might think of me. What I cared about was:

More!

Now!

TWENTY-ONE

ARTHUR

WE WERE OUT BACK AT THE woodpile, me and Bro, splitting logs. Our setup was for Bro to handle the ax while I kept a lookout for snakes. There'd only been the one time a snake had come wriggling out from under the woodpile— a garter snake, I believe Bro said—but it had made a big impression on me. I'd come very close to catching it! Success was right around the corner. In fact, that's my strongest belief. All I needed now was a snake. I sat by the woodpile on high alert.

Bro and Harmony were experts at splitting logs. Elrod had taught them how. "Safety first," he'd said. "Spread your feet shoulder width apart and stand the log up way out in front. That way you'll still have feet when you're done." Which made Bro laugh. Not Harmony. Sometimes she gets an impatient face. That was one of those times.

Splitting logs is hard work but after a while you fall into a nice, easy rhythm, like Bro right now. So there we were, both of us in a nice, easy rhythm, Bro swinging the ax and me sitting comfortably, split logs flying here and there, when I heard a sound. I thought: snake! And got ready to pounce the moment the skinny dude came wriggling into view. But no snake appeared. Instead it was Mr. Smithers, walking up on the plowed path that led from the back door of the inn. If I'd been paying better attention to my nose, I'd have known already. Snakes don't smell of garlic and stale armpit sweat.

Mr. Smithers smiled. "Hey there, Bro."

Bro paused, the ax held high.

"Looks like you know what you're doing with that ax."

"Uh," said Bro, bringing the blade down in one crisp motion and slicing clean through a log. Mr. Smithers picked up the two pieces and laid them neatly on the stack of split logs beside the woodpile. Then he started in on picking up all the pieces and stacking them, too. Like . . . like he was part of our woodpile operation, mine and Bro's. I didn't like that, and it changed my thinking about Mr. Smithers, which had been pretty positive. But even a pleasing smell like garlic and stale armpit sweat will only take you so far in my book.

"Mr., uh . . ."

"Uh, Smithers," said Mr. Smithers, with one of those glints in his eyes that goes with telling jokes. Did Bro get it? I sure didn't.

"You don't need to help, Mr. Smithers," Bro said.

"No problem. I could use the exercise."

That was interesting. For one thing, it meant he was going to get along well with Mom. Maybe he could even sub for me now and then in the exercise department.

"Well . . . ," Bro said, and went back to splitting logs. Mr. Smithers stacked. I did snake duty.

One thing about Bro: He doesn't usually start conversations. So I was a bit surprised when after a while he said, "Hey! Find that wallet yet?"

"Afraid not," said Mr. Smithers, starting a new section of the stack from the ground up. His back was to Bro, but I could see his face. It seemed to change suddenly almost into the face of a different person, one not nearly as nice as my buddy Mr. Smithers. "Kind of a mystery," he said. "And speaking of mysteries, I was interested in what you were saying a little while back."

"Like what?" said Bro.

Mr. Smithers turned to him, and in the course of that turn, his face changed back to normal! We get some unusual guests here at the Blackberry Hill Inn, and I was pretty sure he was one of them.

"The poor fellow—what was his name? Le something or other?"

"LeMaire."

"Right. You were about to tell me that liquor was involved in some way?"

"I was?" Did Bro take his eye off what he was doing for a moment? I thought so. The ax blade almost missed the top of the upturned log completely, hacking off a jagged piece of bark and knocking the rest of the log over like a bowling pin. We have a bowling alley in town and I got to go there once, but it ended up being too exciting and I had to wait in the car.

Bro picked up the log and set it up again. Mr. Smithers's gaze shifted to the ax blade.

"As I remember, we were talking about what LeMaire did for a living and you said it might have something to do with liquor."

"Oh, yeah," said Bro, splitting another log, this time clean down the center, the way Elrod likes it done.

"What made you say that?" Mr. Smithers said.

"Made me?"

"I mean what led you to that thought?"

"Oh," said Bro. "Well, there's the bottle, for one thing."

"What bottle?"

"This old bottle that got found in his room."

"Where was it, just out of curiosity?"

"On the balcony?" said Bro. "I'm not sure." Thwack! Another log, clean through. There were a few beads of sweat on Bro's upper lip now, despite the cold. Fresh sweat.

212

I picked up the scent, of course, and decided that all in all I preferred it to Mr. Smithers's stale armpit smell. But it was a close call.

"Who found the bottle?"

"Deputy Carstairs, maybe?"

"Ah," said Mr. Smithers. "I assume he took possession of it."

"Took it away, you mean?"

"Exactly."

"I, uh."

"Any chance it's still here?"

"Maybe. My mom would know. All I can tell you is it was a real old bottle."

"Oh?"

"Harmony—that's my sister—found out at the library. But you could tell just from looking. It was all covered with dirt."

Mr. Smithers, laying another split log on the stack, somehow missed his aim and knocked over a whole bunch of logs. The sound must have gotten Bro distracted, because on his next swing he missed his log completely, the blade digging into the ground, a little closer to one of his feet than I'd have liked. The laundry room window opened immediately and Mom looked out.

"That's plenty, Bro," she called. "More than enough. Bring in an armload or two." She glanced at Mr. Smithers as she closed the window.

Bro gathered an armful of split logs. I picked up one log—nice and small, no point in working yourself to exhaustion—and followed him, feeling pretty good. I like to pitch in! So did Mr. Smithers, because he grabbed a bunch of logs himself.

"That's okay, Mr.—"

"My pleasure," said Mr. Smithers. And he hurried forward to open the back door for us. Looking back toward the woodpile, he paused. "What's under that tarp?"

"Snowmobile," said Bro.

"Yeah? I've never driven one."

"It's easy," Bro said.

"Maybe you could teach me."

"Sure. But, kind of technically, I have to wait a couple months."

"What for?"

"My next birthday. But my mom could teach you. She taught me and Harmony."

Snow began to fall. A flake landed on my tongue and turned to water. That always surprised me. We carried our loads inside.

Not long after that, we were in the small parlor, Bro building a fire in the fireplace, Mr. Smithers in one of the nice leather chairs, leafing through a magazine, and me on the lookout for snakes. There'd never been a snake inside the house, but somehow I couldn't make myself stop.

"What's with Arthur?" Mom said, coming in with a teapot, cup and saucer, and cookies on a tray.

Bro glanced over his shoulder. "He's just sitting there."

"But he's on edge about something," Mom said. "That's not like him."

"Probably just wants a cookie," said Bro, breaking a stick of kindling in two.

And I did want a cookie. No sense in denying it. But snakes were the reason I was on edge. What if one came down the chimney and landed on Bro's head? Oh, what a horrible thought! I'd never had such a horrible thought in my whole life, and hoped I never would again. I went over to Mom and got close to the cookies.

She bent to pour tea for Mr. Smithers. For a moment their heads were close together, a sight I didn't like. Don't ask me why.

"Enjoying yourself so far, Mr. Smithers?" Mom said, setting the plate of cookies on the end table and straightening.

"You've got a beautiful place," said Mr. Smithers, helping himself, but not me, to a cookie. "Bro was telling me about an old bottle that turned up here in the course of the police investigation that seems to be going on. Is it still around?"

Mom shook her head. "The deputy took it."

"Too bad," said Mr. Smithers. "I collect things like that."

"We found this one online," Mom said. "Supposedly worth two hundred and fifty dollars."

"Very possible. What can you tell me about it?"

Mom explained all about the bottle, Maple Leaf something or other, how dirty it was, the company going out of business long ago, all stuff I might have heard before.

"Sounds legit," said Mr. Smithers. "I'll pay five hundred for it on the spot."

"You will?" Mom said. "But we don't have it, as I mentioned. And I'm not even sure we have a claim to it."

"Maybe even seven fifty," Mr. Smithers said.

Mom's eyes opened wide. "I'll make a quick call." She left the room.

Mr. Smithers went back to leafing through the magazine. Actually just his hands were involved. The eyes, normally moving back and forth during magazine leafing, were motionless and deep in thought. Meanwhile Bro was all set at the fireplace. He lit a match, touched the flame to a twist of paper, and presto! A nice warm fire sprang up. We're good at things like this at the Blackberry Hill Inn. So why didn't we have more guests? Bertha says it's the economy, whatever that is.

Mom came back. "The sheriff's department doesn't know when they'll be able to release the bottle, if ever."

"Too bad," said Mr. Smithers, closing his magazine. "Sounds like a rare collecting opportunity."

"I wish I could help—for both our sakes," said Mom.

Mr. Smithers laughed. He glanced at the fire. "Nice job, Bro."

"Thanks," said Bro.

Mr. Smithers took a bite of a cookie, and then with his mouth full, said, "Happen to notice any unusual markings on the bottle?"

"Excuse me?" said Mom.

Mr. Smithers said, "No, no, excuse me." He finished chewing. "For my terrible manners. I asked if you saw any odd markings on the bottle."

"Like what?" said Mom.

"I don't know," Mr. Smithers said. "Maybe a number or letter?"

Mom shook her head. "You, Bro?"

"Nope," said Bro. "Can we roast marshmallows?"

"When Harmony gets home." Mom picked up the empty tray and started out of the room. She paused at the door. "Have you found your wallet yet, Mr. Smithers?"

"Afraid not."

"Maybe you should check with the sheriff's office. That's sort of the lost and found around here."

Mr. Smithers didn't answer right away. Did I see something like fear in his eyes? Had he just been hit by a thought about snakes? That was my best guess. Finally he said, "It's an idea."

Mom went out. I found to my surprise that I had a cookie in my mouth, and moved to a cozy spot by the fire. This cozy spot was not far from the wine rack. I picked up an interesting smell from that direction, and if I hadn't been busy with the cookie, or just so comfy, I might have gone over to investigate.

TWENTY-TWO

QUEENIE

HARMONY, MRS. HALE, AND I WALKED across the village green, me not walking but lounging in my backpack. The green was snowy white, not green, and snow was starting to fall, slanting on account of the wind.

"Brrr," said Mrs. Hale, pulling her scarf over her face. "I hate the cold. I never used to. Don't get old, Harmony."

"But the other option's not so good," Harmony said.

Mrs. Hale laughed. She was still laughing when a phone buzzed, somewhere deep in the layers of her clothes. Mrs. Hale fished it out. "Hello?" she said. She listened. Her skin got paler, almost matching the color of the snow, except for pink blotches that appeared on her cheeks. "I'm on my way," she said, and tucked the phone back in her clothes, or tried to. It fell on the snowy ground instead.

Harmony knelt and picked it up. "Mrs. Hale? Are you all right?"

"I'm fine," she said, although she didn't look it, in fact seemed to be trembling as she took the phone. "It's Artie."

"Who's Artie?"

"My husband. I told him and told him but he just won't listen."

"Told him what, Mrs. Hale? I don't understand."

"And so did Dr. Hashmi. Why does he have to be so pigheaded? He's had two knee replacements, for heaven's sake! Not to mention the spinal fusion. Plus the—"

"But what did you tell him?" Harmony said.

"That his days of shoveling the driveway were over! A no-brainer. And what does he do, first chance he gets? So now he's slipped and fallen on a patch of ice and they've taken him to the hospital in an ambulance. Could it be more predictable?" Mrs. Hale took a deep breath, the way humans do when they're trying to calm down. "I'll have to take a rain check on this, Harmony."

"Want me to come with you?" Harmony said.

"Thank you, but no," said Mrs. Hale. "This will not be pleasant."

"That's okay," Harmony said again.

Mrs. Hale's eyes misted over. "You're a good girl." She turned quickly and walked away in the direction we'd come from. That left me and Harmony all by ourselves on the village green.

"This is terrible, Queenie."

Certainly true for this Artie character, and possibly for

Mrs. Hale as well, but I myself was undisturbed. Supposing something terrible was happening to Harmony? That would be different.

"I guess we better be heading home," Harmony said.

The wind picked up. I snuggled in close to her. We didn't seem to be heading home, or in fact moving anywhere. No problem. We were just fine like this.

"But," Harmony said after some time, "I was kind of stoked about this visit. If only Arthur hadn't eaten the map!"

True, I supposed, but I didn't want to get into any of the if-only-Arthur-hadn't stuff. Once you started, it never stopped.

"Do you see any reason it could hurt?" Harmony said. "If we went ahead with this visit on our own? Mrs. Hale did say they'd love you at the Evergreen House."

Then how could it hurt? *Giddyap*, I thought, which is what riders say to get a horse moving. Harmony was no horse, but wasn't I . . . sort of a rider? What a pleasant thought! To be a rider of humans!

I kept thinking *giddyap, giddyap*, the whole way to Evergreen House, which turned out to overlook Icehouse Pond, not far from the hockey rink. Evergreen House was really too big to be a house, actually reminded me more of the hospital, where I'd been once, picking up Bro after the broken-wrist-falling-out-of-the-apple-tree incident, which we don't have the time to get into now. The point was that Evergreen House reminded me of the hospital, except for being smaller and white with green trim, instead of all bricks. In short, it looked like a soft hospital, at least to me.

We went inside, entering a nice big room with lots of plants and—what a thoughtful touch!—a caged bird. An old lady had wheeled her wheelchair up close to the bird and was saying, "How's my pretty Polly today?"

Polly said something that sounded a lot like "Get lost." The woman said, "Aren't you a little brat." And they went back and forth like that, with me waiting for the woman to say, "How about I let you out of that cage for a bit?" But she never did, at least not while I was there.

We stopped at the desk, where a much younger woman in a bright-yellow uniform spotted me right away and said to Harmony, "Hi there. You're with the pet therapy folks?"

"Well, I—"

"And what's the name of this cutie pie?" She reached across the desk and—and touched the tip of my nose through the mesh? Did I know her? Did she know me? And the whole rude move was so unexpected that I didn't think of bringing my teeth into play until it was too late.

"Her name's Queenie," Harmony said.

"Oh, perfect!"

"And . . . and we're here to see Mr. Pelter."

"What a fine idea! He hardly ever has visitors. Room one thirty-six in the Garden Wing. Here's our interior plan. And don't be alarmed at anything Mr. Pelter says. On the crusty side at times, but he means well."

"Uh, thanks," said Harmony.

We headed down a hall, Harmony studying the plan, me gazing straight ahead, not in the best mood. Did my eyes have that fierce look? I bet they did. Touched my nose? Beyond belief.

We came to a closed door. Harmony read the number. "G 136." She knocked.

From inside came a man's voice—the voice of an old man, but not especially weak. In fact, it was more of a shout. "What do you want?"

"Oh god," said Harmony, very quietly. Then, raising her voice, she said, "Visitors."

"Visitors? Visitors? What kind of so-called visitors?"

"Yikes," said Harmony, again very softly. And still softly added, "What should I tell him?"

My only thought was to tell him to let Polly out of the cage, but that probably wasn't what Harmony was looking for. Humans, in my experience, often completely miss what's important.

"Uh, Mr. Pelter?" she said.

"Who else were you expecting?"

"Nobody. Sir. It's just that—"

"Are you a kid? You sound like a kid."

"I'm a kid," Harmony said. "My name's Harmony. And I've brought Queenie with me. She's a cat."

"A cat? I like cats. Are you from pet therapy? I've been waiting and waiting."

"We're here," Harmony called through the door. "Which is totally true," she added in the quiet voice.

"Then what are you waiting for? It's not locked. It's never locked, which is just one more blasted—"

Harmony opened the door.

"—reason I'm busting out of here the first chance I get."

An old man was sitting up in bed. He was very small, maybe the smallest man I'd ever seen. But he also had maybe the loudest voice of any man I'd heard, which he was toning down now that we were in the room. He wore a flannel shirt buttoned up to the neck and had what I believe is called a hawk-like nose. In fact, he reminded me of birds, not the kind of birds I usually deal with— like cardinals and robins—but the other kind, the big ones drifting high above. Once I saw one dive down from the sky and grab a rabbit! That gave me a lot to think about.

"Hello, Mr. Pelter," Harmony said.

"Harmony?" he said. "That's your name?"

"Yes, sir."

"What kind of a name is that?"

"My name."

"Oh? Did I ask for a smart answer? Exactly the kind of lip I'd expect from someone named Harmony."

Harmony seemed to get blown back a little, like by a strong wind. But she stiffened, the way she does, and said, "Really, sir? Isn't harmony—with a small *h*—all about getting along?"

Mr. Pelter's eyes—bird-like for sure—got furious. But the expression faded fast, and so did his voice. "I don't see a cat. I was promised a cat."

"Here, Mr. Pelter. In the backpack."

His eyes—suddenly not bird-like but very old—found me. "Well, isn't that a pretty picture? Queenie, you said?"

"Yes, she's—"

"There's a proper name, no two ways about it. No two ways a—" Mr. Pelter blinked, like he was confused. His eyes found me again and he said, "Why is Queenie a prisoner?"

"Oh, she's not. She likes—"

"Then for the love of mercy, let her out!"

Harmony unzipped the mesh covering and I glided out. Where to go? Mr. Pelter's quilt, soft and puffy, looked appealing. Was there even something scratchable about it? Only one way to find out. And the very next moment I was on the bed, sitting beside Mr. Pelter. He smelled like old newspapers, a smell I don't mind a bit.

"Well, well," he said. And, "My, my." Then he reached out and stroked my back with his bony hand. I've felt much better stroking, but it wasn't terrible, certainly better than nothing.

Mr. Pelter glanced past me, at Harmony. "Are you still here?"

"I'm with Queenie," she said.

"So you're staying? Is that it?"

"If it's all right. I'd like to find out about the map."

"Map? I don't have any maps."

"But you did. It ended up in the map room at the library."

"Maps, maps, maps. I don't know about any maps. Everything I have is in this room."

He looked around. There wasn't much to see. Mr. Pelter had stopped stroking my back, but now he started up again.

"I think the map was in a box of your books that got packed up and donated to the library," Harmony said.

Mr. Pelter raised a finger, all twisted and bony. "Donated? Then where's my tax credit?"

"I don't know," Harmony said.

"Ha!" said Mr. Pelter. "That's what you get for trying to pull the wool over my eyes."

"Oh, but I'm not," Harmony said. What was this? She was on the verge of tears, her eyes misting over? Why? I didn't understand. And lucky for me I didn't have to, because Harmony gave her head a quick shake and got back to holding it up and tall, like normal. "The map's important, Mr. Pelter. I . . . I think it got a man killed."

Mr. Pelter went very still. "Where?" he said. "Killed where?"

"Up on the old Sokoki Trail."

"Got more than one killed." Mr. Pelter gazed out the window. Snowflakes slanted down through a gray sky. "Criminals falling out. Like hyenas. But I'm surprised you know. It was a long, long time ago." His eyes closed.

Harmony came closer. "What was a long time ago?"

There was no answer. Mr. Pelter remained sitting up, propped against pillows, but his hand slipped off my back and rested on the quilt. I gave the quilt a slight scratch, just a test. Yes, it would do nicely.

"Mr. Pelter? Are you all right?" Harmony leaned over him. "Is he even . . . yes, he's breathing, Queenie." Harmony pulled up a chair and sat down. It got very quiet in Mr. Pelter's room. That happens in our part of the country, especially on snowy days. There was really not much to hear but the sound of my claws on the quilt; just one front claw, actually, a front claw perhaps blocked from Harmony's view by one of those little toss pillows.

We enjoyed a nice quiet time that came to an end when Mr. Pelter's eyes opened suddenly and he cried out, "No, no, no."

"Mr. Pelter—what's wrong?"

He glanced around wildly. His eyes looked scared. I couldn't help but feel sorry for him. At the same time, he'd interrupted my little amusement. It's only fair to put that in.

Mr. Pelter spoke. His voice, so powerful before, was now high and small, almost like a child's. "Don't go, Daddy," he said. "Not on the lumber road."

Harmony rose and laid her hand on his. The difference in the two hands caught my attention. Harmony's hand was so alive. Mr. Pelter's hand looked like it had been through a long, hard time and was barely hanging on.

"It's all right, Mr. Pelter," Harmony said. "You were having a nightmare."

He turned his head and seemed surprised to see her. She patted his hand. He licked his lips; dry lips, and so was his tongue. All the parts of him: barely hanging on.

"Harmony?" he said.

"Yes."

"With the cat?"

"Queenie's right here."

He turned to me. "Ah," he said. "Beautiful."

Totally true, meaning old Mr. Pelter still hadn't lost it completely. He licked his lips again.

"Are you thirsty?" Harmony said.

"All the time," said Mr. Pelter.

Harmony poured water from a bedside carafe into a glass and gave it to him. His hands trembled. Harmony helped him hold the glass steady and together they brought it to his lips. He drank, then let his head fall back against the pillows.

"I had a nightmare?" he said.

Harmony nodded.

"What was it about?"

"Your daddy, I think. You didn't want him to go on the lumber road."

Mr. Pelter's eyes got a distant look, like he was trying to see far, far away. "But he did anyways."

"He went to the lumber road?"

"Part of his job. But what could he do? I didn't understand. I was a kid, like you."

"What was his job?" Harmony said.

"Truck driver," said Mr. Pelter. "Drove for Foster Mahovlich."

"Mr. Mahovlich?"

"The original Mr. Mahovlich. One who made the money. This was all way back, Depression time. Also

Prohibition. Went together, now that I think about it. The Mahovliches were poor as us, poor as everybody then. But that changed."

"How come?"

Mr. Pelter shot her an angry look. "How come some get rich and others don't? Is that the question?"

"Well, no," Harmony said. "How come the Mahovliches got rich?"

"Didn't I just say?"

"I must have missed it, Mr. Pelter."

"Must have missed it? Don't you know the world's too dangerous for that? Don't you—" Then came a horrible bout of coughing. Mr. Pelter coughed and coughed. I stopped what I was doing with the quilt and moved away. Meanwhile, Harmony held the glass to his lips, got some water into him, and the coughing faded away. He gave Harmony a new sort of look, like he was seeing her in a different way. "What's your name again?"

"Harmony."

"And the cat is Queenie?"

"Yes, sir."

He nodded. "You think I'm crazy, an old old man having nightmares from childhood."

"I don't."

Mr. Pelter tried to take a deep breath, but it ended up

being a sort of shudder. "Prohibition," he said. "That's how the Mahovliches got rich."

"I don't understand."

"No alcohol in Prohibition, Harmony. But only in the good ol' US of A. Up north in Canada they kept on like always. Folks down here still wanted their drink, goes without saying. New York City folks, for example, night-club people, party people, all kinds. Gangsters made big money supplying them. The big problem was getting the stuff into the country."

"Are you talking about smuggling?"

"Didn't you want to know how the Mahovliches made their loot? Smuggling. There's your answer. The liquor came down from Montreal, crossing the border on farm roads at night. My daddy would drive up and meet them on this side—he was the main driver for Mr. Mahovlich. Course there were road blocks on the main roads. But he knew all the back roads, all the old lumber trails. The road-blocks never got set up in the bottom part of the state, so it was pretty much clear sailing south of Mount Misty. The gangsters' truck would meet my dad up there and transfer the load."

"Up on Mount Misty?"

"Lumber road cuts right across the Sokoki Trail, ends up on old Highway Seventy-Seven."

"There's no lumber road on Mount Misty," Harmony said.

"No? Then tell me where it happened."

"Where what happened?"

"All the killing."

"What killing?"

"When it came to an end. The last shipment. The Montreal guy and the New York guy never met in person, up till then. Nobody trusted nobody. Every once in a while the New York guy would come up and stash away payment for the next few shipments. Buried it in a secret place up there, never the same spot twice. Then the Montreal guy would come down and dig it up. Just the two of them knowing the spot. But on the last shipment, just before the end of Prohibition, the two guys met. They ended up in a fight. All by themselves, no one else up there. No one even knew what had happened till my daddy and me found the bodies."

"You, Mr. Pelter? But you were a kid!"

Mr. Pelter closed his eyes. "My daddy was a hard man. Maybe not as hard as some. He wouldn't have brought me up there if he'd known what we'd find. One knifed the other. The other one shot the first. We found them in each other's arms, right outside the cave."

"Oh," said Harmony. "That was awful for you."

A tear appeared in one corner of old Mr. Pelter's eye. He turned his head away. "Awful leads to more awful," he said.

"What do you mean?"

He looked at her. "Nothing you should know."

Harmony shook her head. "I need to know," she said.

Mr. Pelter blinked. "Why on earth?"

"Because of what you said—I think more awful is still happening."

"Don't matter to me. I'll be dead soon enough."

"No you won't."

"Don't be stupid. Nothing inside me works anymore."

And now a tear appeared in the corner of Harmony's eye, too. She blinked it away and said, "I'm sorry."

Mr. Pelter shrugged his puny, bony shoulders. Harmony held out the water glass. He shook his head. Harmony put the glass down and was gazing at it and not at Mr. Pelter when she spoke.

"Did you call the police?"

"Call the police? When my daddy was a smuggler? Got to keep secrets in this life. We went on down the mountain and my daddy told Mr. Mahovlich. Then the two of them went back up there and buried the bodies, Florio and the Canadian. Name's not coming to me."

"Florio was the gangster from New York?"

"Uh-huh. My daddy and Foster Mahovlich buried the both of them and then went looking for the loot."

"What loot?"

"The payment loot—aren't you listening? Payment for the last shipments. Didn't I already say? Florio would come up from New York and bury it somewheres on the mountain. Then the other guy—LeMaire, that was his name—would—"

"LeMaire?"

"—come down from Montreal and dig it up. There was no money—not big money—on either of the bodies, meaning the payment was still in the ground. Fifteen grand. A fortune in those days. But even with the map they could never find it."

"Map?"

"My daddy had a map." All of a sudden he sat up straight. "Isn't that what you come here about?"

"Yes, sir. What can you tell me about it?"

"The Indians got it. That's what I always thought."

"The Indians got the map?"

Mr. Pelter snapped at her. "Not the map! The loot."

"But how do you know?"

"Those woods are in their blood, that's how." Mr. Pelter looked my way. "Can you leave Queenie here with me?"

"No," Harmony said.

Mr. Pelter got very sad. All the energy went out of him and he slumped back down. "Makes no difference," he said very softly. Harmony leaned closer to hear. "Map's only the half of it."

"What do you mean?" Harmony said.

His eyes closed. His lips moved. At first no sound came out but then it did. "Map's useless without the postcard."

"The postcard?"

His lips moved again. "Nobody trusted nobody," he said. "Good night."

Harmony clasped her hands together. "Please don't go to sleep, Mr. Pelter."

Mr. Pelter shook his head, just the tiniest movement. "Leave Queenie," he said, just the tiniest sound.

TWENTY-THREE

ARTHUR

I 'D LIKE TO RENT THE SNOWMOBILE," SAID
Mr. Smithers, coming into the office where Mom and I
were doing the books. She sits at the desk tapping away
at different machines, and I lie under the desk and try to
stay awake. Doing the books is a job, and sleeping on the
job is a no-no. You pick these things up in the business
world.

"We don't actually rent the snowmobile," Mom said.

"How about three hundred for the rest of the day?"

"You seem to be making lots of generous offers, Mr.
Smithers."

"Is that a problem? How about two fifty?"

Mom laughed. "Okay," she said. "Two fifty it is."

"First I'll need a little lesson."

"You've never driven a snowmobile before?"

"It can't be that hard."

"It's not. Where were you planning to go?"

"Just exploring around. The nearby fields, maybe down
to that river out back."

"The ice isn't safe yet."

"Then I'll stay off it. I'm not looking for adventure—just a little peaceful sightseeing."

"Sounds good," said Mom. "Meet you outside in five minutes."

Mr. Smithers left the office. Mom put some stuff in a drawer and then she left, too. Was I in the mood to be alone? Nope. That hardly ever happens. I got up, had a nice stretch, and set off to find some company, heading first for the kitchen, my favorite room in the house.

No one in the kitchen and nothing left out on the counters. Not that I'd even be tempted, but it makes sense to be aware of what's going on around you. Once, for example, there'd been a platter of bacon-wrapped chicken kebabs. Do you know kebabs? They're on sticks, a fact I'd learned that very day. I'd also learned how well bacon goes with chicken. Although is there anything bacon doesn't go with? I thought about that question until I realized I was no longer in the kitchen, but had made my way to the small parlor, also empty.

Where was everyone? I was just on my way back out when I again picked up that interesting scent, coming from behind the wine rack. I trotted over there and squeezed myself into the space between the wine rack and the wall. It was a space where I'd once found a very stale—but still tasty!—corn chip, maybe last spring. I didn't remember it being such a tight squeeze back then. I wondered why. But not for long, because there, partly under the wine rack, lay a wallet. Made of leather—that was the important part. I pawed it out from under the wine rack and picked it up, immediately learning two things. First, this wallet had been in Queenie's possession, and not long ago. Second, it smelled strongly of garlic and stale armpit sweat, which was Mr. Smithers's smell. Had there been some talk about a missing wallet? I had a vague memory of that. And then it hit me, an amazing revelation. This was Mr. Smithers's missing wallet! And I, Arthur, had found it! I, Arthur: the hero of the story! When was the last time that had happened? Possibly never! I pranced out of there with my prize in my mouth. Very soon I'd be hearing, *Good boy, Arthur,* and *What a clever dog!* and *Maybe he deserves a kebab. Or two.*

Kebabs of the chicken wrapped in bacon kind—I almost left that out. But only because of how happy I was, too happy to think straight. Which was the best thing about happiness. Wow. What a thought! Not like me at all. I forgot it immediately.

I trotted down the back hall, and there was Mom, dressed in ski pants and a ski jacket, and pulling on a wool hat.

"Hey there, Arthur, someone's in a good mood." She gave me a closer look. "What you got there?"

The missing wallet! I, Arthur! This was the moment to lay the wallet at Mom's feet and let the good times roll. But crazily enough, I suddenly didn't want to let it go. No reason. I just didn't.

Mom reached out. "That looks like . . ."

I twisted my head away, then shook it from side to side, threw some prancing into the mix. What had gotten into me? I had no idea.

"Arthur! Sit!"

Sit? Mom wanted me to sit? Now, or sometime in the future, some better time when I actually felt like sitting?

"I said sit!"

Really? When I didn't feel at all like sitting, would have much preferred to prance and twist, shake shake shaking that wallet in the back hall to my heart's content? Oh, my heart! So, so content! What about leaping? Should I try a leap or two? Leaps are pretty tiring, and I've found it's hard to get very far off the ground, but I leaped anyway! Leaped and pranced and twisted and shook and—

"Arthur! Play dead!"

I stopped whatever I was doing, rolled over, played dead. Playing dead means you go totally still with all paws in the air. It's okay to keep your eyes open. How else are you going to see?

Mom came forward, crouched down. She took the wallet from my mouth. Well, not right away.

"Come on, Arthur. Let go."

But I just couldn't. Not my fault. My mouth had taken over.

Mom tugged at the wallet. "You're a good boy for finding this, Arthur. Now don't ruin it."

Ruin what? I didn't understand. How I could I ruin anything? I was the hero!

Mom tugged at the wallet. I tugged back. She tugged. I tugged. She—

And then the wallet was in midair, stuff flying out of it all over the place. I went absolutely still, a good good boy, my tongue possibly flopping out one side of my mouth.

Mom started picking things up. I'd spent enough time working the front desk to know what these things were: Cash. Credit cards. What looked like a driver's license. What looked like another driver's license.

Mom stood up straight, examining the two driver's licenses. "What's going on?" she said to herself. Well, to herself and me. "It's the same photo on both of them, but one says Vincent Smithers and the other says Vincent Florio." Mom gazed at me, or possibly right through me to something far, far away. Then she opened the back door. Mr. Smithers, also dressed in a ski outfit, was waiting outside, the tarp already off the snowmobile. He smiled.

"Arthur seems to have found your wallet, Mr. Smithers," Mom said. "Or is it Mr. Florio?" She held up the driver's licenses.

The smile stayed on his face, but now it looked mean. "What a clever animal!" he said. Then with no warning, he drew a gun. My heart started pounding away. "I'm ready for my lesson," he said, and gestured at the snowmobile with the gun.

Mom didn't move. Lesson? I didn't understand. All I knew was that heart of mine, pounding away. Love can make that happen, but so can hatred.

"You seem like a smart person," this bad man said. "Just be smart and you'll do fine."

"You killed Mr. LeMaire," Mom said. Poor Mom! Her body was shaking, although somehow she kept her head perfectly still.

"What a suggestion!" he said. "But if there's any truth to your wild guess, it should make your next decision easy." He gestured with the gun again. "You're driving."

Very slowly, Mom moved to the snowmobile, sat at the controls. The man—Smithers? Florio?—got on behind her, the gun poking into Mom's side.

"Let's go!" he said.

Mom fired up the machine. What was going on? I had no idea. But that gun! Poking into Mom! I charged.

The snowmobile pulled away. I hit top speed and leaped, mouth open, teeth all set to sink themselves deep into the man's leg, let him know what was what. But without even looking, he kicked out with his heavy boot, clobbering me in the face. I fell, scrambled up, fell, scrambled up again, and took off after that snowmobile, running with all my might.

TWENTY-FOUR

QUEENIE

HI!" HARMONY SAID AS WE ENTERED the front hall. She closed the door with her heel, the exact kind of cool move I'd have made in her place. "Anybody home?"

No answer. The inn was quiet.

"Mom? Bro?"

Still no answer. Harmony unzipped the backpack and I dropped down on the floor, landing in my silent way.

"Arthur?"

Arthur wasn't around. I can always sense when he's on the scene, hard to explain how. I just know.

"What was the name of that guest?" Harmony said to me.

That would be Mr. Smithers, the red-bearded dude I didn't like and didn't trust. Harmony went to the desk, checked the guest book.

"Mr. Smithers? You here?"

No answer from Mr. Smithers. Harmony wandered around the house and I followed. We popped our heads into the kitchen, the Big Room, and the small parlor. Harmony eyed the fire, a nice one, a long way from dying out.

"Someone's got to be around," Harmony said.

We climbed the back stairs, looked in Mom's room and then Bro's. And there was Bro, headphones in place, playing video games. His thumbs went wild on the controls. On the screen, horrible monsters were also going wild, hacking each other's heads off and burning villages to the ground.

"Bro? Bro. Bro!"

Bro turned to us, his face blank, like he wasn't really here. His thumbs went still. He took off the earphones. On the screen, a bloody, cut-off monster head was frozen in midair.

"Yo," he said.

"Where's Mom?"

"Downstairs?"

"If she was downstairs, would I be asking you?"

"Maybe."

"Bro! Get it together."

"You're in a good mood."

Harmony stamped her foot. That was a first. "Stop being such a stupid idiot."

"I know you think I'm stupid."

"I don't. You're not stupid."

"Then how come I'm a grade behind you?"

"There's no time for that now! We need to talk."

"About what?"

"All this stuff I found out."

"At the library?"

"No. Well, yes, that, too. But it's mostly about this old man, Mr. Pelter. He used to drive for Foster Mahovlich."

"Foster has a chauffeur?"

"Not that Foster! The grandfather or great-grandfather or whatever he was. The one who started the company. But the point is, Mr. Pelter has information."

"About the map?"

"No. Well, yes. But it's much bigger than that. Mr. LeMaire wasn't even the first Mr. LeMaire killed up on the mountain!"

"Huh?"

"This all goes way back. Back to Prohibition."

"What was that again?"

"Bro! We've been over it. There was a lumber road back then. It must have left some traces. We need to—"

A faint tinkling sound came from below: the bell on the front hall desk.

"Maybe that's Mom," Bro said.

"Why would Mom be ringing the bell?"

"Dunno," said Bro, putting the headphones back on and reaching for the game controller, that little plastic thing with all the buttons. Harmony put her hand on it first.

"Bro."

"What?"

"Come with me."

"Where?"

"Downstairs."

"You want me to go downstairs with you?"

"Yes."

Bro thought about that, but not for long. "Okay."

He dropped the headphones on his bed. We went downstairs, Bro and Harmony side by side, me trailing. Arthur always likes to be out in front. That's one of many many differences between us. Trailing is better, of course, especially for keeping an eye on things. Arthur's life is full of the unexpected. That's not how I roll.

"Prohibition was the no-alcohol thing?" Bro said as we came to the landing.

"Yeah. It turned out to be good for gangsters and smugglers," Harmony said, opening the door that led from our private quarters to the front hall of the inn. "And one of those smugglers was—"

A woman stood at the front desk. Not Mom. She heard us coming and turned our way, the bell in her hand. Not Mom, but maybe around Mom's age. She had dark hair and dark eyes and didn't look happy.

"Hello," Harmony said. "Welcome to the Blackberry Hill Inn. How can we help you?"

246

Which was exactly how Mom wanted visitors to be greeted. Mom and Harmony always got it right, followed by Bertha, Elrod, and Bro, in that order.

"I'm not really . . . ," the woman began. Then she noticed she was holding the bell and put it down. It made a muffled kind of tinkle. Right away I associated that muffled tinkle with this woman, as though that was her special sound. The world can be a very interesting place, especially seen through my eyes. Golden eyes, in case you've forgotten.

"I guess I'd like to speak to the owner," the woman said.

"Our mom's the owner," Harmony said. "She should be back soon."

Bro piped up in that sudden way he has, a sort of burst. "Probably taking Arthur for a walk!"

Harmony glanced at him and nodded. "She's out walking our dog. But we—"

"She thinks he's too—" Bro began.

But Harmony spoke over him. "—can register you if you're planning to stay. I'm Harmony and this is Bro."

Mom thought Arthur was too what? I wanted to know, but the conversation had moved on.

"Got any luggage?" Bro was saying.

"I'm not sure I'll be staying," the woman said. "I just . . . just had to see. See with my own eyes. It's still so unreal."

"Yeah?" said Bro. "What is?"

The woman turned to Harmony. "My name's Melanie Chang," the woman said. "Alex LeMaire was my boyfriend."

"Oh," Bro said.

"Oh, dear," said Harmony.

"And now I'm seeing with my own eyes and it's still not real," Melanie Chang said. She started to cry, very softly, like she was crying to herself. Harmony went to her, touched her shoulder.

"Bro?" she said. "Can you bring those tissues from the desk?"

"What for?" said Bro.

Not long after that, we were in the small parlor, Bro poking the fire, Melanie Chang seated in a comfy chair, a mug of tea on the armrest, Harmony and me on an ottoman we liked.

"Do you know this sheriff?" Melanie said. "Mr. Hunzinger, if I caught the name?"

"Yes," said Harmony.

"He told me he has the . . . the murderer in custody. Matty somebody or other. He let me see him."

"You saw Matty?" Harmony said.

"Well, not directly. It was through a one-way mirror."

Bro jabbed the poker into the fire, real hard. A ball of hot sparks shot up the chimney.

"A one-way mirror?" Harmony said. "The sheriff let you spy on Matty?"

"That part happened so fast," Melanie said. "It was over before I started to feel uncomfortable."

Harmony gave Melanie what I would have to call a hard look, so unusual on Harmony's face.

"Do you know this man, Matty?" Melanie said.

Harmony nodded.

"I'm so confused," said Melanie. "He has a gentle face. I know you can't go by things like that, but . . ." She sipped her tea, holding the mug, not quite steady, in both hands. "But one thing I do know is that Alex had no interest in an old trading post or Colonial artifacts. He never once mentioned any of that to me."

"Did you tell the sheriff?" Harmony said.

"Yes," said Melanie. "But he told me it didn't matter. What mattered was that Matty thought Alex was after the artifacts. The sheriff really wasn't interested in getting too deeply into all that. The important thing was that Matty ran."

Bro jabbed the poker into the fire, even harder this time.

"What was Alex after?" Harmony said.

Melanie shook her head. "That's the question. He was such a complex man. Which was why I . . . I . . ." She turned away.

Bro glanced over at Harmony. He looked angry. Harmony laid a finger crosswise across her lips, meaning zip it.

Melanie looked our way again. "Most people thought Sasha—that's what I called him, although now I'm starting to think of him as 'Alex,' kind of weird—was just a dreamer. He did have big dreams, but he wasn't just a dreamer. The problem was something or other always came along and derailed him."

"What did he do for a living?" Harmony said.

"Various things," said Melanie. "Although not for the past year or so. Alex did have a small inheritance. His family was rich. But that was a long time ago. And the inheritance was dwindling on account of a bad investment Alex made—something about a nickel mine. I never got the details."

"How did his family get rich?" Harmony said.

"They were in the distillery business."

"What's that?" Bro said.

"Whisky," said Harmony.

"That's right," Melanie said. "They did very well during Prohibition but then came a long decline and finally they went out of business. Alex was actually born in a mansion—it's now a museum—but it got sold a few months later, so he had no memories of the place. He hung photos of it on the walls of our apartment."

"I still don't understand why he came here," Harmony said.

"I'm sorry. I'm trying to tell you." Melanie tried to pick up the mug again, but her hands were too shaky and she left it on the armrest. She took a quick glance at Harmony. "Are you the girl who guided him up the mountain? The sheriff mentioned something about that."

"Partway," said Harmony.

"This must be upsetting for you, too."

"We're okay," Bro said, from over by the fire.

Harmony shot him a quick look, possibly reminding him to zip it. "Well, a bit upsetting," she said. "Which is maybe why I want to understand."

"Fair enough," Melanie said. She took a deep breath, pulled herself together. "The LeMaires dealt with a rough family in New York called the Florios. They didn't trust each other, so they worked out a complicated scheme for payment and delivery. Alex spent a long time researching this, hunting through old family records, but evidently the scheme involved a map and a postcard. You needed both to find where the money was buried, but Alex couldn't figure out how it worked exactly. For the very last shipment, at the end of Prohibition, old Mr. LeMaire came down here to collect the money as usual, but old Mr. Florio showed up in person and double-crossed him. No one ever knew the details, but they ended up killing each other and the money stayed buried."

"Fifteen thousand dollars," Harmony said.

"How did you know that?"

"Is it true?"

"Yes and no," Melanie said. "The money was actually paid in the form of small gold bars. In 1932, gold was about twenty dollars an ounce."

"And now?" Harmony said.

"It's about thirteen hundred."

"Wow."

"Yes," said Melanie. "Meaning that original fifteen thousand is now much more."

Bro poked at the fire, more gently this time. "Nine hundred and seventy-five thousand," he said quietly.

They both turned to him in surprise. Well, Melanie in surprise, Harmony in shock.

"Bro? How did you do that?"

"Dunno," Bro said. The fire made crackling noises and then a big log burst into flame.

"Anyway, he's right," Melanie said, "although Alex always rounded it off to a million. Back in the thirties a LeMaire or two went hunting for the gold, and presumably so did the other side, but no one ever found it."

"How do you know the Florios never did?" Harmony said.

"Because Alex came upon one of those postcards. That's what started this whole thing. It was only last month, when a great-uncle died—the last living LeMaire except for him. Alex was cleaning out this great-uncle's cottage up north and the postcard turned up in some moldy box. He got in touch with a Florio descendant—they're still in the nightclub business, apparently. And Vincent Florio was interested in going in together on a new search, fifty-fifty, which he wouldn't have been if they'd already found the gold. He even said he had the map."

"Are you saying the Florios double-crossed the LeMaires again?" Harmony said.

Melanie smiled a small smile, here and gone. "You're way ahead of me." Then her whole face got very sad, and I could hardly believe a smile had just been there. "And way ahead of Alex, too," she said. "He was always a little too clever."

"What do you mean?" Harmony said.

"I don't mean he wasn't smart," Melanie said. "In fact, his IQ was amazing. But I always wondered if it did him any good. Maybe it was the reverse." She sighed. "The truth is he couldn't resist a double-cross of his own. After all, the money was a payment for delivered goods. By all rights the whole thing belonged to the LeMaires. And he was the last one. So it was a kind of redemption, if you see what I mean."

Did they see what she meant? There was no sign of that

on either of the kids' faces. I didn't get it, either, but I also didn't care. What I cared about at that moment was Mom. For no reason I could think of, I was starting to worry about her. And not knowing the reason made it worse.

"But the point is, being too clever, Alex came down here a day early," Melanie went on. "He brought a bottle of whisky from Prohibition days as a gift for Florio, but he also took this old gun that had been in the family. For insurance, he told me. Even though he knew nothing about guns. Still, at the time, I thought he was being clever. Now I see he didn't know what he was doing." Melanie dabbed at her eyes. "When he got here he started poking around. And I guess he somehow found the map on his own—he sent me a text. Does that mean Florio didn't have it after all? There's so much I don't understand. The sheriff told me that no map was found with . . . with his body."

"Did you tell all this to the sheriff?" Harmony said.

"I tried to, but if it's not about Colonial artifacts he doesn't want to hear," said Melanie.

"Because he's got Matty," Bro said. "So what are we going to do?"

"Mom will think of something," Harmony said. "She should be—"

From outside came the sound of barking, the voice very familiar. Arthur has a number of barks. This was the desperate one, usually meaning he was hungry. But was there something else in that bark, something I'd never quite heard from Arthur before? Whatever it was made me worry about Mom even more.

"They're back," Harmony said, and left the room, heading for the front door.

I stayed where I was, keeping Melanie in sight. I was suddenly in a suspicious mood, suspicious of everyone except us, the family. Melanie gazed into her mug. A tear fell from her eye and landed in the tea, made a tiny wave. Bro noticed she was crying and got busy with the fire. Then came Harmony's voice from the front hall.

"Bro? Got a sec?"

"All the time in the world."

TWENTY-FIVE

ARTHUR

THE FRONT DOOR OPENED AND
Harmony looked out. Oh, it was so good to see her!
I was at my wits' end. That's something Bertha
says when everything is just too much, like something's
burning in the oven at the same time the toilets back up.
I'd never understood before, but now I did. Wherever my
wits were, I'd reached the end, maybe even gone past them.

"Arthur?" Harmony said, kneeling down to my level.
"What's wrong?"

Everything was wrong. I panted and panted, couldn't stop.

"Bro?" Harmony called over her shoulder. "Got a sec?"

I heard Bro's voice from inside the house. "All the time
in the world."

"Bro? That means come here."

"Oh."

And a moment later, Bro was in the doorway, too. "Got
a sec means come here? I'm learning something every—
uh-oh. What's with Arthur?"

"He's by himself and he's carrying his leash," Harmony said.

Bro looked around. "Where's Mom?"

"That's the question." Harmony rose, cupped her hands to her mouth, and called, "Mom! Mom!"

No answer. I knew there wouldn't be. Now Bro knelt down and patted my head. "What's the problem, buddy?"

Problems. That was just it. We had problems. Big, big problems. Smithers, Florio—whatever his name was—had taken Mom away! He had a gun! What was he doing to her? I ran my very fastest round and round in little circles, sniffing at the snow, all I could think of to do. Meanwhile, Bro and Harmony were gazing at the road and the trees beyond. There was no one around.

"Mom? Mom?"

I heard something like whimpering. Was it coming from me? I hoped not.

"Harm?" Bro said. "Maybe he wants us to follow him."

They both watched me. "He's never done anything like that before," Harmony said.

They watched me some more. "But he's doing it now," Bro said.

Was that what I was doing? Yes! I just hadn't realized it. Follow me! Follow old Arthur!

Harmony nodded. "I'll tell Melanie we're going."

She went into the house. I was having no trouble picking up Mom's scent. There was plenty of it around. Mom's scent is one of my very favorites. There's something lemony about it that I love. But now it was making me so anxious. How could something I love make me anxious at the same time? When you're past the end of your wits, you can't answer questions like that.

Harmony returned, now wearing her jacket, hat, and mittens. She tossed Bro his jacket and gloves. Bro had decided he wasn't wearing a hat this winter, for reasons I couldn't remember.

"Melanie's staying the night," Harmony said. "Mom can register her later."

"Yeah," said Bro. "Mom'll do it."

Their eyes met. Some sort of strong feeling passed between them. I could sense it, but I didn't know what it was.

"Okay, Arthur," Bro said. "Let's go."

I stopped circling, trotted toward the road, maybe not my fastest trot, but not quite walking, either. At the road I made a turn, headed toward Willard's.

"He's heading toward Willard's," Bro said.

"Mom probably tied him up, went inside for coffee, and he escaped."

"Yeah," said Bro.

"Except why would he go home instead of wait for her?"

"Plus Mom never drinks coffee after noon."

They didn't speak again until we got to Willard's. I picked up speed a bit, heading toward the back of the building, finding the scent of the snowmobile exhaust. On track!

"Whoa," Harmony said. "Come back here, Arthur."

But I didn't want to go back there. I wanted to—

Harmony grabbed my leash. After some changes in position, we all ended up entering Willard's together. Normally I'd have wanted to take my time inside Willard's, nosing around to my heart's content, or even past that. But not now!

Harmony and Bro glanced around the store.

"She's not here," Harmony said.

Which I knew! Why weren't we hurrying? We had to hurry!

"What's with the whimpering?" Harmony said.

"Probably wants one of those bacon chewies," said Bro.

"He doesn't whimper for those," Harmony said. "He just wags his tail super hard. And look at it."

They looked at my tail. For a moment I wasn't sure myself what it was doing.

"Hanging there," Bro said. "Doing zip."

That sounded a bit shameful. I tried to raise it nice and high, but I got no cooperation.

"So what does he want?" Harmony said.

Mr. Willard spoke up from behind the cash. There are three Mr. Willards at Willard's: an old one, a young one—both fans of mine—and one in the middle, not a fan. This was that one.

"What does he always want?" he said. "A handout. And every time it's the same stupid trick. Playing dead. Sheesh. Why can't he—"

"Excuse me, Mr. Willard," Harmony said. "Was my mom in here?"

Mr. Willard screwed up his face. All the Mr. Willards screwed up their faces when thinking was going on. "Depends when you mean."

"Recently," Harmony said. "This afternoon. Within the last hour or so."

Mr. Willard shook his head. "No."

"Let's go," Harmony said, giving my leash a little tug.

"Huh?" said Mr. Willard. "No playing dead?"

"Not today," Harmony said.

That was Harmony, right again. Did we have time for tricks, even great ones like playing dead? We did not. Why not? Because of Mom!

Outside Willard's, Bro said, "Now where?"

"I don't know," Harmony said. "Maybe—Hey! Arthur!"

Had I pulled the leash right out of Harmony's hand? That might have happened. Not good, I know, but . . . but it was because of Mom! I ran around to the back, maybe not actually running on account of how tired I was, although I was certainly trotting my fastest. Right away, I picked up the smell of the snowmobile exhaust and followed it toward the woods behind Willard's. Harmony and Bro came after me, somehow catching up despite my speed.

"He knows something," Harmony said.

I kept trotting, perhaps not my fastest trot anymore, although I was going very fast inside. We came to the opening in the woods where the trail began.

"He's taking us up Mount Misty," Harmony said. "Oh, no—do you think Mom fell? And what would she be doing up here in the first place?"

"Let's not think," Bro said, and he moved ahead of me. All of a sudden the sun came out for the first time in I didn't know how long. Normally when the sun comes out it gives me a nice little lift, but this particular sun was low in the sky, its light glaring here and there through the trees in a way that gave me the opposite of a lift. By the time we started up the first rise, Harmony, too, had passed me, and Bro was no longer in sight. I could still smell him, of course, his smell mixed in with those of the snowmobile exhaust and Mom. And Mr. Smithers—who had turned out to be Mr. Florio, if I was following this right. I'd never liked him under any name.

"Harm!" Bro called down from up above. "Come quick."

Harmony began to run. I tried to run myself, and maybe did a little. Don't forget I'd already been this way today.

I reached the big rock with the tiny sparkles at the first trail split. And there were Harmony and Bro, gazing at our snowmobile, parked off to the side where I'd last seen it.

"She took Arthur on the snowmobile?" Harmony said.

Bro cupped his hands to his mouth. "Mom! Mom!"

No answer. On one side of the split, the trail stayed wide and easy; on the other side it got narrow and steep.

"Which way?" Bro said.

Harmony gazed in one direction and then the other. Finally she looked at me. "Arthur? We need you."

Well, then. I, Arthur, stepped out in front, and I, Arthur led them up the hard part. My tail rose, all by itself. I forgot to mention one other scent I was following, namely my own, which was nice and strong here, both coming and going. It's a fine, fresh smell, by the way, kind of like the inside of our barn mixed with salt and pepper and a hint of bacon grease.

The sun got lower and lower, stopped glaring through the bare branches of the trees. The sky turned red and gold for not a long time and then came shadows spreading across the woods. Meanwhile we were moving fast, and I was sure we were all panting, although actual panting sounds seemed to be coming from only one of us. We climbed

262

higher through the Mount Misty woods, shadows following us up and up. Then came switchbacks that made my
legs even tireder than they already were. I didn't exactly
stop and sit down. It was more like—

Bro turned and looked back at me. "Arthur—stop dogging it."

Whoa! That was going to be hard. Dogging was the only
way I knew. How would Queenie, for example, be handling
this in my place? I had no idea, just knew that this was my
place, not hers. I rose—if in fact I'd actually been on
my butt—and got moving at what seemed like a brisk pace.
Faster than you, Queenie, I thought, *faster than you*. That
had to be true. I was way bigger.

Soon, off to one side, I spotted the small clearing with
the blackened stones in the middle. This was where I'd
found the remains of a PB&J sandwich under a charred
stick. And who was a fan of PB&J? Mr. Florio, who used to
be Mr. Smithers. For a moment I understood everything!
Then came the next moment and I was back to knowing
not too much. And just as happy! Maybe more so this way!

Not long after that, the shadows all joined together and
became night.

"Should have brought a flashlight," Harmony said.

"We didn't know," said Bro. "We'll just have to follow
Arthur's nose."

I moved into the lead, following my nose just as Bro

had suggested. Shapes went by in the darkness, shapes I recognized only because I'd seen them by daylight, like the huge tree stump with the puffball mushrooms on top, and the thick walls of needly trees. Then came the steepest part where the kids had to get down on all fours. And now we were all dogging it! What a great game this would have been if I wasn't so anxious!

By this time we were all panting pretty good. "Know what I'm thinking?" Harmony said in between pants. "We could use a dad right now."

"I can't stand him," Bro said.

They kept going, still on all fours, now grunting a bit with the effort.

"Queenie was his idea," Harmony said after a while.

"So?

"To solve the mouse problem."

"So?"

What was this? Queenie was Dad's idea? Whoa! I had memories of Dad, but they were fading from my mind. I tried to get to the bottom of what Harmony meant, and was still trying when we came to a dark wall rising in the night.

"The cliff," Harmony said.

The steps that were cut into the rock on the lower part gleamed faintly in the night. Bro bent down.

"Harm? Check out the snow here at the bottom of the steps."

Harmony bent beside him. "It's all flattened in a kind of bowl."

Bro rose. "I think Arthur made that."

"He kept trying to climb up?" said Harmony.

"And falling back down."

That was exactly it! How had they figured that out?

"But he got up the last time," Harmony said.

"Did you give him a treat?" said Bro.

"Yes."

"Then that's the answer. The point is, when he couldn't get up, he came back to get us."

"But Mom would never go up there and leave him behind," Harmony said.

They both tilted up their heads and shouted, "Mom! Mom!"

First there was silence. Then their own voices came down from above—from that old old old Sokoki Trail, if I was getting this right—now sounding far away and scared.

"Mom! Mom!"

TWENTY-SIX

QUEENIE

WE SAT BY THE FIRE, ME AND THIS
Melanie person. I could have joined her on
the nice comfy chair, but I didn't want
to be that close to her unhappiness. If Mom or one of
the kids is unhappy, that's somewhat different. Melanie
was a stranger. I take my time with these things. After a
while her head tipped sideways and she fell asleep. Very
slowly her face lost that unhappy expression. It didn't go
all the way to happy, instead remaining neutral. Melanie
turned out to be pleasant to look at. I looked at her and was
even contemplating joining her after all, when I suddenly
remembered my wallet. Perhaps not my wallet originally,
but my wallet now.

I headed over to the wine rack, slipped behind it, and—
surprise, surprise. No wallet. One or two quick sniffs and
the mystery was solved: Arthur had been this way and now
had my wallet, unless he'd lost it or buried it and of course
forgotten where, both strong possibilities. I considered

revenge, but quickly realized I didn't even know Arthur's whereabouts at the moment. Hadn't he just been barking at the front door? In fact, where was everybody? I went very still, almost my stillest, and listened carefully. No one was home, no one except me and Melanie. Gazing at the fire and thinking deep thoughts, had I lost track of events? That can happen, especially to those who aren't simpleminded.

I glanced at the window over the wine rack, saw it was almost fully dark outside. Yes, events had passed me by. I know what you're thinking: their loss. And I agree. But still, I found myself a little anxious. I glanced over at Melanie, still sleeping by the fire. No help there. Wasn't this the time of day when everyone was around? I smelled nothing cooking. One part of me wanted to stay right there, hidden behind the wine rack. Another part of me wanted to slip down to the basement and check out the mouse situation. The two parts were still fighting it out when I heard the front door open. At last! Mom!

But . . . not so fast, Queenie. Those approaching footsteps were not the footsteps of Mom, Harmony, or Bro; not those of Bertha, Elrod, or Big Fred; not even those of Dad, who hadn't been around in some time and was not missed, at least by me. These footsteps were vaguely familiar, meaning I'd heard them before but not often. I stayed behind the wine rack, peeking through the bottles.

A big man appeared through the open double doors of the parlor, one of those big men with a barrel-like upper body and sticklike legs. No one had switched on the lights, but firelight gleamed on his huge gold watch and flickered across his face. It was Mr. Mahovlich.

He scanned the room, his gaze passing right by me and finally fixing on Melanie, asleep in her chair. Mr. Mahovlich came into the room, walked quite close to her, and switched on a small table lamp. He peered down at Melanie for a moment or two, then stepped back and coughed into his hand, not a real cough but the kind humans make to let you know they're around. As if I didn't always know already.

"Uh, miss?" he said.

Melanie's eyes flew open. She saw Mr. Mahovlich. "Oh!" she cried, and put her hand to her chest. "You . . . you scared me."

He gave her a smile that looked warm, if you didn't know him. "Nothing scary about me, miss. Name's Harrison Mahovlich, but everyone calls me Bud."

Interesting. I'd never heard him called anything but Mr. Mahovlich.

"I'm a good friend of the family," he went on. "Wonderful family. Wonderful inn, a credit to the town. Are you a guest?"

"Yes," said Melanie, sitting up straighter. "At least, I think so. I haven't actually registered yet." She glanced at the window. "Goodness, what time is it?"

Mr. Mahovlich—he'd never be Bud to me—checked his gold watch. "Ten minutes to seven."

"I can't believe how long I've . . ." Melanie peered past him toward the darkened front hall. "It's so quiet. Where is everyone?"

"I was going to ask you that," said Mr. Mahovlich.

"I don't know."

"Well, nothing to worry about. Mind if I join you?"

He pulled up the ottoman, actually the ottoman I thought of as my own. I made a mental note—I'm a great maker of mental notes—to do something to the ottoman after he left, soon I hoped, that would Queenie-ize it once more.

"Are you here for the skiing, miss?"

"Melanie, please," she said. "And no, no skiing. I . . . I'm not really here for any of the usual reasons."

Mr. Mahovlich smiled. "Now you've got me curious. But no need to explain. You know what they say about curiosity."

Not that again. Where does this idea come from? How can it be stamped out? A problem for later. At the moment I thought it was important to focus on the here and now.

"Speaking of cats," Melanie was saying, "there was a beautiful one here earlier." She looked around. "I don't see it."

A beautiful one? I came to a decision: Melanie was all right.

"Don't know about a cat," said Mr. Mahovlich. "I do know they've got a dog."

As for Mr. Mahovlich, he was worse than I'd thought.

"I haven't seen a dog," Melanie said.

"A big fat mutt," said Mr. Mahovlich. "Don't recall the name."

Which proved there's good in everybody, even someone like Mr. Mahovlich.

"But as for my reason for being here," Melanie said, "I suppose you could say it's part of the grieving process." Tears filled her eyes. "Even though I hate that term—like there's a checklist with boxes to tick off."

"So sorry," said Mr. Mahovlich. He put his hands together. "Someone close to you died?"

"My boyfriend," Melanie said. "He . . . he was murdered."

"Murdered?"

Melanie nodded. "It happened here. I don't mean right here in this inn, but up on a nearby mountain."

"Mount Misty?"

"That's right. You probably heard something about it."

"Just rumors," Mr. Mahovlich said. "Not much in the way of hard facts."

"Hard facts appear to be scarce right now," Melanie said.

Mr. Mahovlich seemed to be waiting for her to continue, but she stared into the fire instead.

He cleared his throat. "Was his name LeMaire? I think that's what it said in the paper."

She nodded. "Alex LeMaire. I call . . . called him Sasha."

"Always liked that name," said Mr. Mahovlich.

Melanie looked at him, perhaps sizing him up for the first time. I got the feeling she decided he was a nice guy.

"Do you know the local sheriff?" she said.

"Hunzinger? I've met him."

"What's he like?"

"Couldn't really say," Mr. Mahovlich said. "Why do you ask?"

"I met with him," Melanie said. "He told me he's made an arrest."

"I heard something about that."

"The sheriff is convinced that he's got the killer, a man named Matty Comeau."

"I heard that, too."

"He believes it was all about Colonial artifacts and a lost trading post."

"Yeah?"

Melanie nodded. "His theory is that Alex wanted to dig them up. Comeau's an amateur archaeologist and hates when random people come to dig in the woods. They met on the mountain and Comeau . . . did what he did."

"Do I hear some doubt in your voice?"

"Alex had no interest in Colonial artifacts. He never mentioned them once to me."

"That's puzzling," said Mr. Mahovlich. "Then why did he come here?"

"It's a long story," Melanie said, "and quite complicated. I was telling those very nice kids—Harmony and Bro, I believe?"

"That's right," Mr. Mahovlich said.

"I was telling them all about it when they suddenly had to go."

"Oh?" He glanced around. "It is a bit of a surprise that no one's here. Any idea where they went?"

"Harmony said they'd be back soon."

Mr. Mahovlich rose, went to the back window, gazed out. "Isn't there usually a snowmobile parked out back?"

"I have no idea."

He went on gazing into the night. The moon had risen and its light turned his face to stone.

"Is there someone who does know the sheriff?" Melanie said. "Someone he'll listen to?"

"I'd have to think," said Mr. Mahovlich, and from my angle I could see that he was thinking hard. "What is it that you want the sheriff to hear?"

"Well, for starters I think he should look into the whereabouts of a man named Vincent Florio. Where was he when Sasha was killed?"

Mr. Mahovlich went very still, as though he really had turned to stone. "Go on," he said, his voice soft. Soft in a way I didn't like one little bit, but Melanie heard it differently.

"Thanks for being a good listener," she said. "This is about long-ago events—and I don't know how much of it, if any, is true. But doesn't Sasha's death . . ." She fell silent.

"I like a good story," Mr. Mahovlich said, turning to her with a smile.

"All right, then," said Melanie, and she started in on what I'd already heard, all about maps, postcards, gold.

"A good story for sure," Mr. Mahovlich said when she was done.

"How much truth do you think is in it?" she said.

"I'm in no position to judge," said Mr. Mahovlich. "But what I can do is try to rustle up your hosts."

"That's very nice of you."

"No trouble," said Mr. Mahovlich, moving toward the door. "Enjoy your stay."

He went into the hall. I slipped out from behind the wine rack and followed him in my silent way, past the desk and to the front door. He opened it and stepped outside. I was right at his heels, not a place where a human is apt to spot you. We walked to his car. Mr. Mahovlich opened the driver-side door. He got in. And so did I, gliding onto the floor of the back seat. Mr. Mahovlich turned the key and we were off. Did I have a plan in mind? Possibly not, but I can improvise if necessary, just another one of my talents.

TWENTY-SEVEN

ARTHUR

THE SOUND OF *MOM! MOM!* DIED away, and then the night went quiet. The kids looked at each other. Something unspoken passed between them. That happens with me and my kind all the time! Just another reason to love the kids.

Bro turned to me. "Think you can get up there, big guy?"

I did! For sure! Piece of cake! Even if cake's not my favorite, although I don't turn my nose up at it. I don't turn my nose up at any kind of food. That wouldn't be polite.

"Okay," Bro said. "Go!"

When Bro says go, I go. Unless I'm extra tired or feeling lazy. And right now I wasn't either of them. I gave my head a quick shake, just to bat my ears against the side of my face, get the blood flowing, and charged up those steps cut into the rock face and beyond those steps, scrambling up the steep slope, clawing my way past the rusty handholds until—

But no.

Somehow—maybe a bit tired after all, especially in the legs—I lost my grip and tumbled backward, off the cliff and down. Plop. I landed flat on my back in the snow. Didn't hurt at all. I popped right back up. At least in my mind. In actual fact, it might be more accurate to say I continued to lie on my back in the snow, paws up, mouth open. I decided to pop back up the very first moment I felt ready.

"Got a treat on you?" Bro said.

"No."

"Then we'll have to carry him up."

"How?" said Harmony.

"We'll get him on my shoulders."

"You could get hurt."

"What else can we do?"

Harmony faced back down the trail, the way we'd come. After a very short distance it vanished into the darkness. "We could go for help."

"How long would that take?"

There was a pause. Then Harmony said, "You're right."

"About what?"

"Just kneel down, Bro."

Right then the moon appeared over the trees, and everything close by was silver and clear. Bro knelt.

"Come on, Arthur," Harmony said. "Up we go." She patted Bro's shoulder.

What was this? Some new game? Normally, getting taught a new game involves treats. That was the best part! I've been taught many games, including fetch and shake, and actually managed to learn one, namely playing dead, so I knew that we always started with, *Hey, Arthur, want a treat?*

But was I hearing that now? No. Meaning I was supposed to do what? Climb up on Bro's shoulders or some crazy thing with no treat in the picture? I tried to make sense of that and failed.

"Arthur!" And now Harmony was snapping at me? That had never happened before. We were in a bad way. "Up! Now! We need you to find Mom."

Mom? I'd forgotten about Mom. Mom! The next thing I knew I was up on Bro's shoulders, hanging on tight as he climbed the steps and then pulled us up the cliff face, handhold by handhold. I could feel how hard Bro was trying, could feel the strength that was suddenly in his body, almost the strength of a man. He never grunted, not even once.

We reached the top. Bro crawled up onto level ground, his chest heaving. Harmony scrambled up beside us. She touched Bro's arm, so gently he might not even have felt it.

"Ready?" she said.

"Yup."

Bro started to rise. I stayed where I was, clinging to his shoulders. I was pleased with learning a new trick and was pretty sure a treat would be coming eventually. I trusted Harmony and Bro. But more important, I realized that I liked riding around on Bro's shoulders. Why hadn't I thought of this before? Was there any reason most of my future traveling time couldn't be spent like this? What was the word riders always said when they wanted a horse to get moving? I was still trying to come up with it when Bro said, "Arthur! For god's sake!" He gave a quick twist and then I was on the ground.

"Concentrate, Arthur," Harmony said. I had no clue what she meant. Then she added, "Find Mom."

I got that. Mom!

I sniffed the night air, picked up Mom's lovely scent right away, and kind of over it in a way that's hard to describe, the garlicky, stale-armpit smell of Vincent Florio. Also, mixed in with the Mom part was the smell of human fear. Poor Mom! I picked up the pace.

I'd been this way before, of course. We were back on the old Sokoki Trail. It looked different in the moonlight, but it smelled the same, and part of that same smell was the smell of bear, not recent. Had all the bears gone to sleep by now, that long wintry sleep of theirs? I'd heard something about it and hoped it was true.

I led the way, up the steep rise through the Christmas-type trees and onto the flatter part, moving sideways across Mount Misty. I felt something strange and alive under my paws. It had to be the strength of Mount Misty, even if that made no sense. The kids' boots crunched in the snow. I myself was silent as a cat. Whoa! Forget that last part.

We crossed a frozen stream, tiny moons reflecting on the ice, and moved onto deeper snow. There were two sets of footprints in this snow, big footprints and not as big footprints. No one said anything. We picked up the pace, even though it was already picked up plenty. The little tower of stones appeared, and after that the frozen waterfall, like a silver curtain in the moonlight. And soon we were back in the tiny, snowy meadow. Had I found some sort of map around here? I had a faint memory of that. Whatever it was couldn't have been important. I did have a clear memory of me and Harmony discovering the body of Mr. LeMaire, hidden under the tangle of branches on the other side. But the scents I was following—Mom's and Florio's—did not lead that way, and neither did their tracks. Instead those scents and those tracks took a sharp turn and entered some thick woods, thicker than any we'd seen so far, blocking almost all the moonlight. But I could see that the tracks were now in single file, the big foot-prints often blotting out the small ones.

"Whoever it is is walking behind her," Harmony said.

"Yeah," said Bro.

"Like in a bad way."

"I know."

They were right. It was a bad way. I'd never liked Mr. Florio, not even back when he was Mr. Smithers. Now just the thought of him was making me angry. I hardly ever got angry. When was the last time? Oh, yeah. The sheriff and Mr. Immler. What had that all been about? I tried to remember but too many pieces were missing.

Meanwhile we'd come to a spot where the woods opened up a little on one side, almost like the beginning of some sort of snowy lane, although it was too overgrown with bushes and small trees to be an actual lane. Mom and Mr. Florio had gone that way, so we did, too. With me in front, just in case you're like me and forget important things from time to time.

"This must be where it cut across the Sokoki Trail," Harmony said.

"The old lumber road?" said Bro.

"That's right," Harmony said. "The smugglers' truck—"

"The Mahovlich truck?"

"Yeah, driven by Mr. Pelter's dad. It came right through here. We must be—"

At that moment we heard—I don't know what to call it: a shout? a call? a cry? But a human voice, a woman's voice, in fact, the voice of Mom.

And then we were running, not easy in the snow, but I hardly noticed. Me first, then Harmony, then Bro. But soon it was Harmony, then Bro, and then me. That was very bad. Was this a good moment for barking? Just a sharp-ish bark or two to remind the kids of right and wrong? Yes, it probably was a good moment, but could I run my fastest—which involves a lot of panting—and bark at the same time? No. Therefore I decided to save my barking for later. Saved barking turns out to be sharper and louder when I finally let loose, a fact you might not know.

And now we had moonlight again. It turned the foot-prints black in a world of silver. Those black prints led off the old lumber road, down through a grove of trees and toward a dark, rocky outcrop, jutting from a steep slope. As we got closer I saw something strange: The prints went right into the rocky outcrop and disappeared. Then I saw the tall, narrow opening in the rocks.

"The cave," Harmony said in a very low voice. "Where Mr. Pelter and his dad found the bodies."

We stood outside this cave. Harmony and Bro exchanged another of those looks of theirs, where something silent gets said. I came very close to understanding what it was.

But there wasn't quite enough time. We stepped through the narrow opening and into the cave.

At first it was so dark I couldn't see a thing. Then my eyes pitched in—they're pretty good at night, maybe better than yours—and I made out a widening space that led to a downward-sloping tunnel. A bluish-white light flickered at the tunnel opening, faded away, came back. It reminded me of the phone lights old folks at the inn used to help them read Bertha's breakfast menus, back when we had guests. We walked toward that flickering light.

Then, from out of the tunnel, came Mom's voice. "You've got this completely wrong." After that there was a . . . I didn't know what to call it. A slapping noise? Something like that. None of us liked that sound, not one little bit. I could tell by how fast we moved into the tunnel, Harmony first and me last, even though I always like to be first. Plus it's my job! This was no time to be doing it badly. I squeezed in front the first chance I got, which was when the tunnel opened up into a sort of dim room with damp, rocky walls, a high rocky ceiling, and a dirt floor.

The only non-dim part was a cone of light that came from a cell phone, propped up on a jumble of rocks. In that bright bluish cone was a terrible sight. Mom was sitting on the cave floor. Florio stood over her. He had a gun in one hand. Her nose was bleeding.

282

"I'm running out of patience," Florio said.

Mom looked up at him. Her face looked strange and blue. "I can't help you," she said. Poor Mom. She must have been so scared. But did her voice tremble? Not a bit!

"See, I think that's a lie," Florio said. "When I met with LeMaire down in the meadow—"

"Where you killed him," Mom said.

Florio raised the gun, rested the barrel gently on Mom's head. "I hate interruptions. Understood?"

There was a long pause. Finally Mom said, "Yes."

Florio withdrew the gun. "When I met with LeMaire I was sure he had the map. No point in coming up here without it. You need both—the map and this." He took something from his pocket, held it in the light for Mom to see. The postcard. He shook his head and laughed. Human laughter almost always sounds good to me. This was one of those times it didn't. "The Depression's the reason for all this mumbo jumbo. Those two old guys didn't trust anyone. The map was supposed to show the different hiding spots in the cave. The postcard indicated the one for the last shipment. LeMaire wanted to meet me because he thought I had the map." He smiled. "Which I did not, but I kind of let him think the opposite. And then I came up here early, just in case he was pulling a fast one. And wouldn't you know? He showed up early, too. Didn't that mean he'd somehow found the map on his own? That was the subject of our little discussion in the meadow. He denied he had the map, but I wasn't convinced. A smart guy maybe, but not cut out for this kind of thing. He didn't want to be searched, forcing me to . . . subdue him." He held up the gun. "With this, actually. The butt end. I never intended . . . something permanent. And after all that, it turned out the map wasn't on him. Know what I think?"

"I hope," said Mom, "that you think it's not too late to stop all this."

"You can't be that stupid," Florio said. "My take is that LeMaire heard me coming and hid the map somewhere. I couldn't find it, but guess what I'm betting."

Mom didn't answer.

"I'm waiting," Florio said.

"I don't know what you're betting," Mom said.

"I'm betting your daughter found it."

And now, for the first time, Mom's voice lost its steadiness. "You're wrong."

"Nice try," Florio said. "See what you think of this plan. First, I'm going to search you. Then, if the map's not on you, you'll . . . wait up here, so to speak, while I go down for a quick confab with your daughter."

"No," Mom said.

"No?" said Florio. "You're not being given a choice."

"But none of that will do you any good." Mom's voice was trembling badly, no doubt about it. I'd never been more upset in my life. "There is no map. Not anymore."

Florio raised his voice, all the way up to a shout. "Not anymore? What is that supposed to mean?"

Somewhere up above a rock shook loose and fell to the cave floor with a thump. It landed near Florio's feet but he didn't seem to notice.

"WHAT DO YOU MEAN?"

Another rock fell. Florio got way too close to Mom, sort of surrounding her.

"ANSWER ME!"

Mom tried to shrink away from him but there was nowhere to go. She looked up and said, "There is no map. Arthur ate it."

"Arthur? What are you talking about?"

"Our dog."

Florio smacked Mom across the face with the back of his hand. That was my last clear memory of things for a while. I saw red! Even though there was no red to see. I saw red anyway and charged at Florio. Were Bro and Harmony with me? I believe so, but I was in the lead. No one could have kept up with old Arthur at time like that.

Florio heard me coming and spun around my way. With shock on his face! And fear! Both very nice to see. He raised the gun. I launched myself at him.

BANG!

Something hot whizzed through the fur on my shoulder. An instant after that, I got him by the gun arm, sinking my teeth in deep. He cried out. I sank my teeth in deeper. And he cried out again. We wrestled around on the floor and then, oh, no! He kicked me in the stomach, real hard. I rolled away, just out of the cone of light.

BANG!

This bang was followed by the zing zing zing of the bullet bouncing off the rock walls of the cave. Then came something hard to describe. The cave didn't like that bullet zing zing zinging off its walls. It let out a kind of low roar and then a big part of the ceiling tumbled down, missing me, the kids, and Mom, but burying Florio under a huge, stony, silent pile.

Oh, no! But not missing Mom after all. That was just me, wishing for happiness. The truth was that Mom was buried, too, all except for her head. Her eyes were open so wide. How frightened they looked! This was the worst thing I'd ever seen. A great howling rose up from deep inside me.

Harmony and Bro rushed over to Mom. Without a word, they fell down on their knees and started grabbing rocks, some of them really big, and flinging them away like they were nothing. And how they worked, their hands just blurs—like they were one mighty being, digging, digging,

digging. In what seemed like forever, but maybe was no time at all, they had Mom free and on her feet.

"Mom, Mom, are you okay?" Harmony said.

Mom slowly patted herself, tried a few little leg movements. "I seem to be," she said. "Oh, kids!"

The next moment we were all together, hugging and crying, except for me. I wasn't part of the hugging and crying, but I made up for that by being the most all-together of anybody.

Mom moved toward the phone—quite steady on her feet—and shone the light around. Dust rose from the rock pile and another stone or two came loose from the ceiling. But in the pile itself nothing moved or made the slightest sound.

"Let's get out of here," Mom said.

We turned to go.

"Wait," Harmony said. "What's that?"

She pointed at the wall. A flat stone, not much bigger than a book, had fallen away, exposing a hole.

"That's a letter painted on the rock in there," Bro said.

"*C*," said Harmony.

We went closer, peered into the hole. Down at the bottom was a golden glow.

"The gold bars," Bro and Harmony said, speaking as one. Bro reached in and pulled out a gold bar, about the size and shape of the French bread loaves Bertha sometimes bakes, possibly called baguettes. We were all admiring it when a voice came from the opening to the tunnel.

"Well, well."

Mom shone the light in that direction. And there stood Mr. Mahovlich. He had a light, too. He shone it on us, the rock pile, the gold bar.

"What are you doing here?" Mom said.

"Same as you, I suppose."

"I don't understand."

Mr. Mahovlich spotted Florio's gun, lying on the floor, quite close to him. He picked it up and said, "Maybe you won't have to." He held the gun loosely, not pointed at us, and not exactly not at us, either. "We had family tales about the gold, but I doubted them. So congratulations. I owe you." The gun came up, slowly and still not definitely in our direction. I was a little confused. I'm sure my confusion would have cleared up in no time, but before it could, a small, dark shadow came streaking through the air. This shadow seemed to land on Mr. Mahovlich's side or arm. He cried out in pain, whirled away, trying to shake off the shadow.

"ARRRGH!" Mr. Mahovlich cried out again. He lost the gun, which came spinning our way. Mom scooped it up. The shadow separated from Mr. Mahovlich and glided over to us. This shadow turned out to be Queenie. She sat down and yawned.

TWENTY-EIGHT
QUEENIE

THIS HAD BEEN AN ENJOYABLE outing, even exciting at times, yet I was ready to be back home. I'm no expert on human behavior— I have other things to ponder—but I expected that they were thinking the same thing. So why didn't Mom now shoot Mr. Mahovlich and be done with it? Instead we had a complicated conversation going on, lit by cell phone light, with Mr. Mahovlich talking real fast.

"I hope you don't misinterpret my actions, Yvette," he was saying. "I dropped by the inn to check out room availability for some friends of mine, and ended up talking to your guest—Melanie, I believe? From what she said, I pieced together the possibility that you and the kids—" He raised his free hand in a little wave to Harmony and Bro; his other hand was wrapped in a scarf he'd been wearing, a scarf that now dripped blood, the drops black in the cell phone light, a very displeasing sort of light to my eyes, by the way, although the sight of his blood made up for that.

"—you and the kids," he was saying, "might have gone up here. Not really safe at night, in my opinion, so I thought, as a friend and neighbor, that I'd come check. And I think my fears were borne out. Whose gun is that?"

Mom held the gun firmly, pointed down. "We can get to that later," she said. "Do you really expect me to buy your story?"

"I sure hope so," said Mr. Mahovlich. "It's the whole truth and nothing but." He gazed at Mom in an innocent way that reminded me of Arthur, who was currently standing between Harmony and Bro, his tail wagging maniacally.

Mom gazed back. "And you brought Queenie with you?"

He turned to me. I could feel him thinking hard. "Well, yes. She seemed to want to come."

What was this? He hadn't known I was with him to the very end, that sweet moment of biting and blood.

"Queenie did?" said Harmony.

"At least so I thought," Mr. Mahovlich said. "I even imagined she liked me." He held up his scarf-wrapped hand and laughed the kind of laugh I believe is called rueful. "Evidently not."

A few moments passed. I got ready for Mom to shoot Mr. Mahovlich but that wasn't what happened. Instead she gave him a long look, not friendly, and said, "Let's go home."

We left the cave—an odd sort of place and in the end disappointing. Wouldn't you expect to find mice in that kind of setup? And yet there was not a single trace of mouse. Arthur took the lead until he got tired, which was almost immediately. Bro carried him the rest of the way. Harmony carried me the whole time, although I wasn't the least bit tired. I gazed at the moon and felt wild, through and through.

Oh. The gold bars. Mr. Mahovlich carried those over his shoulder, wrapped in a sort of bundle he made with his sweater.

"Can't deny I haven't had thoughts about the gold," he said when we were back in the front hall of the inn. "The charities I'd leave it to, supposing the gold came into my hands. That kind of thing."

"There by the grandfather clock will be fine," Mom said. "You can keep the sweater."

"What are we going to do with the gold, Mom?" Harmony said the next day.

"Let's buy a place in Hawaii and take up surfing," Bro said.

"Whoa and double whoa!" said Harmony. "Can we?"

Mom laughed. "First we have to make sure it belongs to us. It looks like at least some does—the state may get a portion. As for what we'll do with it, Matty's coming over later. I thought we'd discuss it with him."

"Huh?" said Bro.

"We were thinking, Matty and I," Mom said, "about a small archaeology museum dedicated to Colonial history in these parts."

"You mean we're giving it away?" Harmony said.

"Not all of it," said Mom.

"Will there be enough left for the place in Hawaii?" Bro said.

"It doesn't have to be on the beach," said Harmony.

And there was more about Hawaii, beaches, and surfing, but I lost interest. Did a call come in about the arrest of the woman possibly named Mary Jones, possibly of Brooklyn? I paid no attention.

A little later, I ran into Arthur on the stairs. We both paused and gazed at each other. It was an interesting moment.

By the day after that, the inn was packed with guests, most of them media people. Media people turned out to be just what we needed. They paid top dollar for everything, Bertha said, and ate and drank huge amounts. In fact, a party started up, and then we got snowed in so it went on for days. Arthur played dead 24-7 and scarfed up so many treats he could barely move. The whole house shook with fun and noise and laughter. Not my kind of thing at all. I spent most of my time down in the basement, doing what I do, and simply being, well, me.

ACKNOWLEDGMENTS

Many thanks to Mallory Kass, my very talented editor at Scholastic, and also to Rachel Griffiths for encouraging this project in its early days.

ABOUT THE AUTHOR

Spencer Quinn is the pen name of the Edgar Award–winning novelist Peter Abrahams. He has written many books for younger readers, including the *New York Times* bestselling Bowser and Birdie series, and the Edgar-nominated Echo Falls series. His novels for adults include *Oblivion*, *The Fan* (made into a movie starring Robert De Niro), *The Right Side*, and the *New York Times* bestselling Chet and Bernie mystery series. He lives with his wife, Diana, and dogs, Audrey and Pearl, on Cape Cod, Massachusetts.

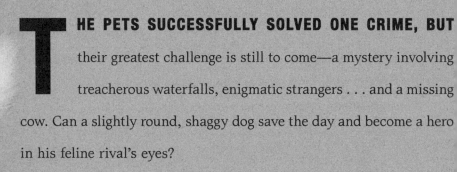

CAUTION CAUTION CA

THE PETS SUCCESSFULLY SOLVED ONE CRIME, BUT their greatest challenge is still to come—a mystery involving treacherous waterfalls, enigmatic strangers . . . and a missing cow. Can a slightly round, shaggy dog save the day and become a hero in his feline rival's eyes?

FIND OUT IN THE NEXT
QUEENIE AND ARTHUR
NOVEL, COMING SOON!

CAUTION CAUTION

ON